Look for More Titles by Cassandra Chandler

LINGERING TOUCH

Other Works
CRAFTING A WRITER'S LIFE: Building a Foundation

Coming Soon

The Blades of Janus
PERIHELION

The Department of Homeworld Security
Nothing to Declare

Export Duty

The Department of Homeworld Security
Book Nine

Cassandra Chandler

Copyright Page

Export Duty
The Department of Homeworld Security, Book Nine
Copyright © 2019 by Cassandra Chandler
Print ISBN: 978-1-945702-40-2
Digital ISBN: 978-1-945702-29-7
Edited by Eliza Sinclair

First eBook edition: March 2019
First print edition: March 2019
10 9 8 7 6 5 4 3 2 1

cassandra-chandler.com
P.O. Box 91
Mission, Kansas 66201

Dedication

For Rob P. — an amazing healer.

Don't miss out on any of the alien action.
Subscribe to Cassandra Chandler's newsletter at
cassandra-chandler.com!

Chapter One

Lily was heading into a trap. She felt it in her bones as her truck bounced along the uneven gravel and sand that led to the small bungalow at the end of the lane. When she was close to the house, she turned off the engine, but didn't get out of the truck. She needed to plot out contingency plans.

The place looked so innocent. Powder blue stucco—chipped in a few places—and flower boxes in every window, bursting with colorful plants. Palmetto fronds hung above the driveway, as if personally shielding whoever came to this oasis from the oppressive afternoon heat. The house itself was tucked back into a canopy of white pines and oaks.

A bug flew in through the open window. Lily shooed it away.

"Why did she have to build her house on the edge of the Everglades?" Lily mumbled.

A small wisp of a woman stepped out into the shade surrounding her house, her white hair fluffed out around her head like a cloud. Her eyes were as blue as the sky above—just like Lily's.

"Lily? Is that you?" The woman stretched out her arms and made grabby hands. "Come on over here, sweet pea!"

Lily slid from her seat, dragging her purse with her. By the time her feet hit the ground, she was being pulled into a huge hug.

"Nana Lillian," she said. "How are you?"

"I'm just fine." Nana laughed, then pulled back and squeezed Lily's arms. "Let me look at you."

"It's only been a month."

"I used to see you every week."

Lily pushed down a huge pang of guilt. Tried to, anyway.

"I know," she said. "Things at the warehouse have been so busy. Helping mom has taken up—"

"Quit fussing, I didn't mean anything by it." Nana waved a hand at Lily, then hooked her arm into Lily's elbow and headed for the house. "You take things so seriously. I just wanted you to know I missed you, that's all. I have plenty of company out here."

As if summoned by her words, a glaring of cats raced out from the house's open door.

Drat.

The cat treats Lily had brought along for them were still in the glove box. She'd get them later.

Lily was pretty sure she'd learned every word for a group of cats since Nana retired. Clowder, clutter, pounce, glaring. Nana's house seemed to spawn the things.

Meows and purrs greeted them as the cats wove around their feet. Lily nearly tripped a few times, but Nana kept her upright.

"You're not doing your yoga, I see," Nana said. "Skipping your practice isn't good for your balance—on many levels."

"For someone who isn't trying to guilt me, you sure are hitting my weak spots."

"Oh, honey." Nana leaned into Lily's side. "You know I'm here to help. Just...*way* out here." She moved her free hand in an arc, accenting her words. "Do you like living in the old loft?"

"I do. But you didn't have to give it to me."

"Pshaw. I can do what I want with what's mine. And now it's yours."

They stepped into Nana's kitchen, a cooler breeze wafting through the open doorway. Lily wasn't sure how Nana managed to keep her house so cool, but she wasn't about to complain. She really needed to get the AC in the truck fixed.

Nana poured iced tea into two glasses from a sweating jar. She wiped the condensation on her neck when she was done and let out a little sigh, then handed a glass to Lily.

"Let's sit on the back porch," Nana said. There was a gleam in her eye that Lily only saw when Nana was onto a very special find. Treasure hunts, she called them.

Dread curled in Lily's stomach. Was this where the ambush would happen?

Nana had said she wanted to introduce Lily to someone, and wouldn't say more—aside from reassuring Lily that she wasn't trying to hook her up with anyone. A lifetime of experiences pushed back against the promises.

The last time Nana had tried to "introduce" Lily to someone, she'd said, *"You don't have to marry him, just have a little fun!"*

Nana and Lily's mom were both free spirits when it came to...pretty much anything. Lily wished she had half their confidence and spontaneity.

Neither woman shied away from going after what they wanted, whether it was in the boardroom or the bedroom. Lily was the weirdo who always thought things through and had to have a million contingency plans before venturing into something new.

She followed Nana to the porch, a weird mix of relieved and disappointed to find all four wicker chairs empty. Well, except for the cats.

"Shoo. Shoo." Nana cleared two of the chairs of cats for them. Once they were settled, she said, "Is your mom handling things okay with the business?"

"Of course. Everything's fine."

"Then why are you having to help her so much?"

"I get it. I'll try to make it out here more often." Guilt aside, Lily really did miss their visits.

"Honey, you've got to loosen up a little. Yes, I love spending time with you, but I'm more concerned that you're focusing on the business too much. Is that really what you want to do with your life?"

"How can you even ask? You built that company from nothing. I'm going to take it over eventually, and—"

"Who says you're going to take it over? I built it because it's what I wanted to do. Your mom took over because it's what she wanted. That doesn't mean you have to."

Lily felt her heart skip at the thought. She'd spent her childhood playing among the boxes of rare goods her Nana somehow managed to trade for, buy, or dig up herself. It was like growing up in a museum where Lily could play with the exhibits—as long as they hadn't been sold yet.

But she wanted to make a difference. To help people. She was already brainstorming ideas of how to use the family's contacts and resources for altruistic pursuits when the company passed to her.

"I do want to learn the business," Lily said. "And I'll make it my own when it's time."

"Of that, I have no doubt. But the universe is much more vast and interesting than even I ever imagined. Life on Earth is short, and I want you to enjoy it."

Life on Earth?

That was…weird. Lily wrote it off as something Nana had picked up from one of the books she was constantly reading. They both took big drinks of their tea, then set down their glasses on the wrought iron table between them, moving at the same time. Sharing a look, they laughed at the synchronicity they so often enjoyed when they were together.

Insects droned loudly from the surrounding woods. With the shade of the trees and the porch roof, it was much cooler than the drive out had been. A cat jumped onto Lily's lap, but she immediately evicted it. Even with the shade, she couldn't stand the extra heat it was putting off.

"They miss Cyan." Nana chuckled.

"Who's Cyan?"

"She's who I asked you out here to meet. Actually, she should have arrived by now." Nana stood and shouted, "Cyan?"

Lily let out a nervous laugh. Cyan must be a new cat. Although, Lily couldn't guess why Nana wanted to arrange a special introduction for this one. Maybe it was super feral, and Nana needed help taming it. Lily was pretty good with animals.

"Cyan!" Nana called again.

"I'm sure she'll come around when she's hungry," Lily said.

"Hungry? Is that a vegan joke?" Nana slapped her thigh. "Oh wait. You don't know where she's from yet."

"Who *does* know where they all come from. I swear these cats are growing on the trees out here."

Nana laughed. "Cyan's not a cat. She's my yoga partner. That's her mat over there."

She pointed at the corner of the living room that was visible from where they were sitting. A couple of yoga mats were rolled up and propped against the wall, including a new one that looked like a child's mat. Maybe somebody with kids had built a house nearby?

Nana would be a great influence on any child's life. Lily really did miss coming out for visits. As much of a pain as it was to make the long drive, the conversations always left Lily with plenty to think about, and doing yoga under the evergreens was an amazing experience.

"We meet out here every day around this time and I give her lessons," Nana said. "Her tail gets in the way sometimes, but we work around it."

"Her tail?"

Oh no.

The lovely image of Nana mentoring a little girl evaporated in a slew of memories that set Lily's teeth on edge. What the heck was Nana messing with this time?

Once, Nana had saved one of her cats from an anaconda that someone had released into the woods. It had scared Lily within an inch of her life to see the pictures Nana took with the Rangers who came to pick up the snake and relocate it to a nearby sanctuary. The thing was enormous.

Nana had insisted it not be put down. She'd said it was only following its nature. Then she'd found a sanctuary that had an outreach program to teach people about the dangers of introducing invasive species into new ecosystems. The sizeable donation she'd made had no doubt helped their decision to take in another snake.

"Cyan is such a sweetie," Nana said. "You're going to love her. Maybe she's nervous."

"Nana, what is Cyan, exactly?"

"She's a Vegan."

"A 'vaygun'?"

Nana walked a few paces toward the trees, shouting, "It's okay, dear. I just invited my granddaughter to meet you."

"A vaygun?" Lily repeated.

"Yup." Nana laughed. "It's the funniest thing. You remember Sarah over at the Old Oak restaurant?"

"Of course," Lily said.

Sarah wasn't someone Lily would easily forget. She had built her business around a treehouse in a huge oak tree. Sarah lived in the loft at the top of the treehouse, and ran a health food restaurant out of the lower level. There was a deck below, with picnic tables that could easily be moved around for community events and outdoor exercise classes.

Lily had been trying to work up the nerve to ask Sarah for help with the changes Lily wanted to make to her family's business. Sarah had incredible business acumen, and seemed closer in temperament to Lily than Lily's mom and Nana were. Plus, Sarah knew a ton about health and wellness. Lily had already imagined the two of them brainstorming alternatives if a group of people needed medicines that weren't available.

Yeah... Lily really thought things through too much. She needed to work on that.

"Well, Sarah advertised that she was expanding her menu to include vegan options," Nana said. "But she capitalized it on the sign, making it 'Vegan'."

What the heck is a vaygun?

"Okay... So, Cyan is a vegan?" Lily exaggerated the "vee" sound when she said the word.

"No, a Vegan." Nana mimicked Lily's emphasis, but stuck with her mispronunciation.

"I've never heard that word before," Lily said.

"I don't doubt it. There aren't many Vegans running around on Earth yet. But there will be." She gave Lily a quick wink before turning back to the forest.

Lily's nerves pulled tighter. "Nana, what are you talking about?"

"My friend Cyan. She's a little lizard person from the Vega system."

The ground seemed to tilt beneath Lily's feet.

"You're going to love her," Nana went on. "We've been having the best conversations. This world is so new to her, and she's curious about everything. It makes you appreciate things in a way you'd never expect."

Lily's throat was so tight, it was hard to speak.

"Nana..."

"She must be invisible," Nana said. She cupped her hands around her mouth. "You can drop your cloaking field, dear. I promise, Lily is a friend."

How suddenly could dementia come on? Nana was in her seventies, but her mind had always been sharp as a tack. She was healthier than most people Lily's age. She took care of herself.

The guilt Lily had been barely fighting off finally won, falling on her in crushing waves. It had been a month since she'd visited. That must have been enough time for Nana to lose her mind.

Nana loved her independence—and living out in the country. But there was no way Lily could leave her out here by herself anymore.

Lily walked over to the woman she'd idolized for as long as she could remember, and gently rested her hand on Nana's arm.

"Nana, we need to talk."

Chapter Two

"I must speak with you."

Rin turned toward the small voice coming from the other side of his exam table. He had to step around the table to see who had spoken.

"Hi, Cyan," he said. "How are you today?"

The tiny Vegan glanced around the room, her tail twitching behind her as she hunched over. The spines that ran from the middle of her head all the way to mid-tail were standing straight up. Her green scales and the bluish stripes crossing over her back were a bit paler than usual, the contrast against the silver bands of her exosuit not as pronounced.

Normally, she had a tendency to wring her hands together when she was upset. Today, she was twiddling her long fingers.

"If I didn't know better, I'd say you're nervous," Rin said.

"Shh. I mean…" She stood straighter, running a hand along the spines on her head and smoothing them back. "I have no reason to be nervous."

"Uh-huh. What can I do for you, then?"

"I have need of your…specialties."

He racked his brain for what she might mean. There was no way she needed a field medic. The technology on the Vegan Life Ship was beyond anything Rin could offer in the makeshift med-bay he was setting up for the new Department of Homeworld Security base in Florida. Hell, just her exosuit made his skills completely obsolete. And he barely knew anything about Vegan anatomy.

"You'll have to narrow it down for me," he said. "Do you mean my devastatingly good looks or my whimsical charm?"

Cyan huffed a breath from her nostrils, her lips shut tight. "Neither of those."

"Damn. I should have known. You only have eyes for Kyle."

"I am not here to speak of the beautiful Tau Ceti."

"Tau Ceti-human hybrid."

"He does not like being called a hybrid."

She stood straighter, her spines lowered and arms at her sides. Rin may have pissed her off, but at least she didn't look frightened anymore.

"My apologies," he said.

"I do wish Kyle would not always uses the emitter Nika designed that masks his natural green coloration. It is so—" Cyan shook her head briskly, then stamped her tiny foot. "You are distracting me on purpose."

"So, my ability to be distracting isn't what you need? Because the only 'specialty' left that I can think of that you don't already have access to is my skill at Earth swearing. And if you need that… Well, that's fucking weird."

Cyan snorted again, but this time it sounded like a laugh. Rin was learning how to read the little lizard people's expressions. Cyan was by far the sweetest of them.

Her eyes suddenly crinkled shut and she arched her neck and back. Her spines stood on end, quivering. She held her arms out straight in front of her. It almost looked like she was having some sort of seizure.

"Cyan?" He was just reaching for her when she let out a huge sneeze.

The sneeze alone wouldn't have concerned him as much, although the build-up to it had been pretty frightening. But her scales turned a pale orange and her green-blue stripes faded to white. She shook her head as her colors gradually turned back to normal.

"Holy shit," Rin said. "You need a doctor."

"You *are* a doctor."

"I mean a Vegan doctor. What the hell was that?"

"Shhh!" Cyan turned in a circle, looking all around the room. When she finally stopped, facing him again, she was wringing her hands. "My exosuit indicates that there are no recording devices in this room. Is that correct? No surveillance equipment of any kind?"

"Yes, and there never will be. This is an Earth-style

medical examination room, and I'm following their ways in respecting people's privacy. I'm just tricking it out with Sadirian technology. But now *you're* distracting *me*. What just happened?"

"I am unsure. That is why I have come to you."

"You need to be seen by a Vegan doctor."

"My symptoms do not cause me much discomfort and they are intermittent. I do not wish to bother the doctors aboard the Life Ship."

"Cyan..."

She went on as if he hadn't interrupted. "And besides, they are all busy preparing for the arrival of the *Reckoning*."

Rin's stomach twisted. Knowing the Coalition warship was on its way had everyone on edge. For him, it was a special level of hell.

Clara was on board.

The last time they spoke, he told her that he loved her. She told him his feelings marked him as inferior.

In her mind, because he loved her enough to tell her how he felt, the genetic engineering process that created him had failed. She didn't even call him a glitch. To her, he was an aberration. He was surprised she hadn't reported him for culling.

For a while afterwards, he thought that meant she'd been trying to protect him. That she cared for him. After a few more cycles on the *Reckoning*—with her utterly ignoring his existence—the only conclusion he could reach was that she didn't think he was worth the effort.

Thank the stars General Serath had approved Rin's request to transfer to the *Arbiter*.

"Rin, is your attention diverted?" Cyan tugged on a fold of his T-shirt that was just within her reach. "I did not mean to disturb you."

"Shit. I'm sorry, Cyan." He shook his head. "I shouldn't have let myself get distracted like that."

"There is no shit," she said, patting his forearm. "It is a stressful time. I will address the issue on my own."

"No way. I'm here to help." As much help as he could, anyway. "When did these symptoms start?"

She paused for a moment, then said, "A few weeks ago."

"Weeks? Why didn't you come to me sooner?"

"I did not wish to burden anyone."

"A change of that magnitude is… Well, in a Sadirian or a human, it would be a huge deal. I'm not as familiar with Vegan physiology."

"It is also abnormal for us."

"Well, let's start by downloading your exosuit's biometric data," he said.

Her scales turned a dull olive green and she clasped her hands in front of her, bowing her head. "There is no biometric data."

"No data. How is that even possible?"

"This was a mistake," she said. "I… I will handle the

issue on my own."

"Cyan, wait." He clasped her shoulder gently.

Something was going on. Extenuating circumstances that made her want to keep secrets. But secrets could be deadly when it came to medical treatment. He had to find a way to put her at ease enough that she would confide in him.

When she turned back to face him, he said, "On Earth, many doctors take an oath, pledging themselves to care for their patients. Part of that is a thing called 'doctor-patient confidentiality'. Their patients know that whatever they discuss with their doctor will be kept private, unless doing so would create a threat to others. It's a wonderful philosophy, and one I've sworn myself to."

Cyan cocked her head to the side in a singularly reptilian manner. "The Coalition would never allow such an oath from a soldier."

"Do you seek approval for everything you believe in with all your heart?"

She was silent for a moment, regarding him with her golden eyes. "In our time together, I have come to consider you a friend."

Warmth spread through his chest at the thought. "I'm honored. I consider you a friend as well."

"Perhaps it would be best for me to show you..."

"Show me what?"

"What I believe to be the source of my symptoms. But

you must promise me that you will tell no one."

He lifted one hand, and said, "I swear it."

"The others have often said you have adapted to Earth swearing quite well." Cyan cocked her head at his hand, then lifted her own. "I accept your swear."

"That's... Nevermind." It didn't seem the time to explain the Earth gesture.

"We will need a vehicle."

"A vehicle?" he asked, surprised.

"You do not have an exosuit, and the journey will take us many miles away. The distance is too great for you to traverse on foot."

Where the hell was she taking him?

He didn't want to press the matter, fearing she'd balk at letting him help. "Okay, then," he said. "Let's go talk to Ari."

"It is better we approach Nika. Ari is busy helping Sarah and Cerulean train Kira in the use of her new exosuit."

"Everybody's busy nowadays," Rin said. "And I'm not sure it'll make a damn bit of a difference." He muttered the last words under his breath, but Cyan reached out and squeezed his hand.

"The work we do here is important," she said. "And it will make more than a damn bit of difference. This planet is our homeworld now. All who are here. We will fight to protect it."

He smiled down at her, trying to feel her optimism. The

Vegans *would* fight to protect Earth. But the Coalition soldiers stationed along with him...

He didn't know what would happen to them when the High Council turned its full attention on the Department of Homeworld Security. He only knew it wouldn't be good.

"Right now, my main concern is protecting *you* from whatever's going on with this sneezing," he said.

Cyan smiled at him, increasing her grip on his hand. She closed her eyes, and the silver bands that wrapped around her body like a second set of stripes began to expand. The metal lines running along her spine lengthened, as well as the ones near her feet, lifting her body higher.

He'd seen Kira, Sarah, and Ari practicing with their exosuits under Cerulean's studious gaze. Rin had never been able to watch one function from so close. Knowing everything else it could do, this shouldn't impress him as much as it did.

When Cyan opened her eyes again, her suit had become a reptilian-shaped metal chassis that lifted her several feet off the ground. Neither would have to reach up or bend down to hold hands.

"Shall we?" she asked.

He laughed and nodded. "Sure."

The vehicles were kept in a garage a few buildings over from the med-bay. *Clinic.* That was the Earth word. Vay, their cultural programmer, would be all over him if she heard him use "med-bay" instead. Fortunately, that was unlikely since she was in Montana with her Earthling bondmate, Henry, and the pair of mated Lyrians who had adopted him.

Rin wished the team could have stayed together, but this was Sarah's home, and she didn't want to move. Since she was the link between Earthlings and the Vegans, they didn't have much choice but to set up a second base. Plus, the ecosystem in Florida was perfect for the Vegans' reptilian physiology.

Unless there's something in the environment that's affecting Cyan...

Rin needed more information. Better to not cause alarm by sharing the concern prematurely.

The main door to the garage was wide open. It was big enough for a small ship to navigate through. Inside, he could hear aggressive, discordant Earth music blasting away. Nika was definitely around.

"Nika?" Rin called. He glanced down at Cyan in time to see silver bands morph from her exosuit, stretching up to cover her ears. "Not a fan, huh?"

"The music is quite exhilarating, however the volume is a bit high."

"Agreed. Nika!" he shouted.

He thought he heard someone say, "What?"

"Turn down the music," Rin yelled.

He glanced around for the source of the sound and noticed a set of speakers that looked like they had originated from an Earth factory, but had been heavily modified. Cyan squeezed his hand and tugged on his arm when he started toward them, urging him to stay put. She smiled, then pointed at the equipment, stretching out her hand and lowering her arm. The volume went down.

"I have got to get one of those exosuits," he muttered.

"It is quite a commitment," Cyan said. "They can not be removed."

"What, like ever?" He looked her over more carefully and noticed that there were still silver bands attached all along her body, even with some of the metal morphed into the scaffold that lifted her higher up.

"Ever," Cyan said.

Rin filed that bit of data away, just in case he ever had to work on someone wearing one. Surgery could be tricky if there was damage to an area covered by the device.

"Who's messing with my music?" Nika appeared behind one of the vehicles, holding a tool that crackled with golden energy. The tight spirals of her black hair were pulled into a ponytail and a smudge of…something was streaked across her dark brown cheek. A huge grin split her face when she saw them. "Okay, you two are adorable."

"Yeah, we get that a lot, right, Cyan?" Rin winked at his companion, but could tell she was worrying again. Her tail whipped back and forth, and she started to pull her hand away. He held on gently, and gave her fingers a squeeze, trying to reassure her.

Cyan let out an indignant snort through her nostrils. "Some species do seem to find our smaller stature reminiscent of their offspring."

"I didn't mean any offense," Nika said. "Now I'm curious, though. What are we like to you?"

Cyan cocked her head to the side and made a clicking noise. "I can not speak for all Vegans, but I find you…soft and squishy."

Rin suppressed a laugh.

"I had to ask." Nika clicked off her tool and set it aside. "What can I do for you today? Or are you just out for a stroll?"

"We're here for a vehicle," Rin said. "Cyan needs a little help with her field work studying the wildlife in the area."

"Right, you're a biologist, like that Earthling, Henry." Nika rifled through a drawer in one of the work tables that lined the interior of the building. She pulled out a set of metal keys and tossed them to Rin.

If he'd been expecting it…he still wouldn't have caught them. Nika's throw went wide, the keys hurtling closer to the door than to Rin.

"Oops," Nika said.

Cyan lifted her free hand quickly, stretching out her fingers. The keys stopped mid-air, then floated over to Rin's waiting palm.

Nika let out a low whistle. "I have *got* to get one of those."

"They're quite a commitment." Rin winked at Cyan again, and she let out a low series of hisses that sounded almost like giggling. He smiled at her and said, "Let's go."

Chapter Three

Tears blurred Lily's vision as she drove down the road that led away from her Nana's bungalow. Their conversation had not gone well, to say the least.

She loved Nana, and only had her best interests at heart. That didn't stop Nana from kicking Lily out at the height of their argument.

"I can't believe you think I'm crazy," Nana had said.

She'd seemed genuinely hurt. But how else was Lily supposed to explain away Nana's new yoga buddy, the lizard lady from outer space?

Lily wiped her eyes clear with the back of her arm. She doubted she'd encounter anyone on this back road, but didn't want to risk not being able to see another—

"Crap!"

A small offroad vehicle sped past her as she turned a corner flanked by thick trees, nearly clipping the front of her truck. Lily swerved out of the way. It was gone before she had a chance to honk, but she'd caught a quick glimpse of a man inside who seemed to be in the middle of an argument.

That wasn't the weird thing, though. The weird thing was that no one else was in the car with him. And he'd been sitting in the passenger's seat. The driver's seat was empty.

"What the hell?" Lily said. "Now *I'm* hallucinating."

He was headed toward Nana's. There was no other place the road led to.

What did that guy want with Nana? Who even *was* he?

Before Lily could think better of it—or think about what she was doing at all—she slammed on the brakes, her back tires swinging the truck in a semi-circle on the loose gravel road. A cloud of dust obscured her view. She sped through it, heading back the way she'd come.

The car had just pulled into Nana's driveway when Lily arrived. She parked behind it and killed her engine. Whoever was inside didn't seem to have noticed her. They turned off their vehicle, but kept arguing.

Lily had just slid out of her truck when their doors opened. No one exited the driver's side, but the man she'd seen earlier stepped out of the passenger's door.

Lily's breath caught in her throat. She'd caught a glimpse of short dark hair as he'd hurtled past, but she hadn't seen how gorgeous he was.

He had light brown skin, a strong jaw, straight nose, and raven-wing brows over equally dark eyes. His shoulders were broad, and his T-shirt hugged a chest so defined, she could see the outlines of his pecs through the thin fabric.

"That's the last time I ever let you drive," he said. "Earth vehicles are *not* the same as piloting—" His eyes widened as he saw Lily. "Shit! I mean, hi."

He cast a devastating smile at her, complete with dimples. It was almost enough to distract her from the nonsense he'd been spouting.

Almost.

Lily crossed her arms. "'Earth vehicles'?"

He stammered for a few seconds, then said, "It's a... figure of speech."

She arched an eyebrow at him. "Maybe on the International Space Station."

He laughed, deepening the dimples. Her stomach did a little flip, which she pointedly ignored.

"Who are you?" she asked.

"I'm Rin. Doctor Rin." He took a few steps forward and extended his hand.

Some women were into backs or butts. Some liked gravely voices. Lily was into hands.

His were perfect. Long, tapered fingers, strong palms. She clamped her arms tighter against her chest to keep from reaching for it.

"You're a doctor." She pointedly stared at his cargo shorts and hiking boots.

He followed her gaze. "Looking for a white coat and a stethoscope?"

She shrugged. "Or something."

"I'm a field medic, actually."

"A psychiatrist would be more help," she muttered. She wasn't buying his story for a second. "Making a house call all the way out here?"

"I guess so."

"Cyan?" Nana's voice broke into the conversation. "Oh, Lily. You're back."

Nana stood just outside the door to her house, hands crossed over her own chest as she glared at them. Half a dozen cats ran out around her feet, bolting toward a nearby oak tree.

"Doctor Rin" stiffened at the sight of them, his jaw dropping. Lily supposed that many cats could be intimidating.

"Did you want to call me crazy some more?" Nana said.

"Nana—"

Nana gestured at Rin. "I see you even brought along some backup."

"What, me?" Rin glanced around. "I'm just here to… make a house call."

"What are you—" Nana paused, then clapped her hands together. "You must be Rin."

"Yes." He flashed that megawatt smile again.

"You're here to help Cyan," Nana kept on, her voice rising with excitement.

"Yes. I mean, no." He laughed uneasily, glancing at Lily and shaking his head. He shifted toward Nana. "I'm here to help *you*. Remember?"

"I don't need any help," Nana said. "It's poor Cyan that has the problem."

The cats started meowing loudly, as if they were trying to join in on the argument. Lily glanced over to see what looked like the whole glaring circling the tree. They must have cornered something up there.

A huge orange marmalade tabby scampered up the trunk, all the way into the high branches. Lily wasn't sure they'd support his weight.

She pushed down a feeling of misgiving. The ground below was mostly sand, but if the cat fell from that height, she wasn't sure the soft-ish surface would make a difference.

"Quiet down, you," Nana yelled. "Or you won't get any of the treats Cyan always brings along."

"Nana, please," Lily said. "There's no such thing as lizard people."

"Right." Nana gestured to Rin again as she approached them. "Next thing you know, you'll be telling me aliens aren't real."

"Whoa," Rin said. "Everybody knows aliens aren't real." He blew out a breath and rolled his eyes at Lily. The whole gesture was so exaggerated, it was almost comical.

"Then what are you?" Nana asked.

"I'm a perfectly typical Earthling." He hurried to correct himself. "I mean *man*. A human man. From Earth."

"Cyan told me all about you." Nana thumped him on the

chest with the back of her hand. "You're a soldier from the Coalition of Planets, assigned to Earth. A Sadirian from the Gamma Cygni system. Own it."

"Coalition of Planets?" Lily said. "How are we even having this conversation?" She turned to glare at Rin. "Are you behind this? Because if you are, I swear to God, I'll—"

"I really am a doctor," Rin said. "And I'm only here to help."

He sounded so earnest. Lily was usually a pretty good judge of character, except when it came to guys she was interested in. This one was seriously distracting her with his gorgeous looks, charming demeanor, and perfect hands.

"If you really are a doctor, help me deal with this," she said. "Is it some sort of sudden onset dementia or something?"

"Don't you dare drag him into our argument," Nana said.

"Look, I think we all need to just calm down and take a moment to breathe." Rin took in a deep breath, then let it out, lifting and lowering his arms like a conductor trying to rein in a wayward ensemble. When Lily and Nana just glared at him, he said, "Nobody wants to breathe?"

"We *are* breathing." Nana and Lily shouted the words at the same time.

The cats let out a chorus of indignant "mrak" sounds, and Rin jumped again. He took a step closer to his car, staring at the glaring as if he'd never seen a cat before.

Great. Now Lily was going off the deep end, too.

"I know you're not supposed to go around telling people you're an alien," Nana said. "But this is my granddaughter. She's named after me. We're close enough, we don't keep secrets."

"We're not talking about secrets here," Rin said. "We're talking about—"

"Lizard people," Nana said.

"Yes." Rin nodded, then looked confused and suddenly shook his head. "I mean, no. Not lizard people." He let out an exasperated sigh, then turned toward Lily. "I need to speak with my patient in private, if you don't mind."

"As a matter of fact, I do mind," Lily said.

At that moment, one of the cats let out a huge yowl. Lily heard what sounded like a sneeze from the giant oak. She looked over just in time to see the orange cat fall from the top of the tree.

"Oh no," Lily said.

She started running toward it, but stumbled and fell onto her face as something appeared out of thin air next to the falling cat. Spitting sand from her mouth, Lily craned her neck up to see a tiny figure hurtle through the air, curling itself into a ball around the orange tabby.

Green scales covered the creature's skin, including its long tail. It had metallic silver stripes in regular intervals banding its body as well as running down its spine. Greenish-blue stripes that looked more natural streaked across its skin.

Cyan-blue.

"Oh my God," Lily said.

The lizard person—*lizard person*—kept sneezing as it fell. It still managed to twist itself around into an upright position, holding onto the cat fiercely as it did. Orange coloration spread over its body, and its stripes turned white just before the pair hit the ground.

"Cyan!" Nana yelled.

Rin made it to the tree first, but only barely. He crouched down next to Cyan, and said, "Are you injured?"

"My exosuit protected me, but..." Cyan lifted the cat, holding it up with her little green hands under its armpits.

The cat was almost as tall as the lizard lady, stretched out like that. His body was lax, dangling from her grip, and he was purring so loud that Lily could hear it from several feet away.

"He's fine, sweetie," Nana said. "Don't worry."

Cyan let out a huge breath, bowing her head. Then she held the cat up higher, as if she was showing it off to Rin.

"This is Freddie," Cyan said. She pulled the cat closer, hugging him against her chest and pressing her cheek against his. "He is my favorite."

Lily felt something stirring in her chest. It burbled up and came out as a laugh that sounded hysterical even to her ears.

Everyone looked over at her, lying face down in the

sand. When she pictured how she must look to them, it only made her laugh harder.

"Is *she* all right?" Cyan asked, cocking her head to the side as she stared at Lily.

Nana waved at Lily dismissively. "She's fine."

Lily didn't feel fine. She didn't feel real. None of this did.

"This has to be a dream," Lily said. "Nana, a lizard lady, and a hot alien doctor. Yeah. This is a dream."

"I better check on her," Rin said.

He approached slowly, as if Lily was a wild animal he didn't want to set off. He eyed her as warily as he'd eyed the cats. Maybe he really *had* never seen a cat before.

That thought brought on another bout of laughter. Rin paused, glancing over his shoulder at Nana and the lizard person.

"Go on," Nana said. "She won't bite."

Rin's spine stiffened, and when he looked back at Lily, his face was pale. That only made the laughing fit worse.

Blonde, blue-eyed, and tiny. Lily had never considered herself intimidating before.

She pushed herself onto her knees and watched Nana go into the house. Cyan was right behind her, dragging along "Freddie", who was still purring up a storm. As Lily finally regained some composure, Rin knelt in front of her, just like he had with Cyan earlier.

"*Are* you all right?" Rin asked.

"I don't know." Lily wiped at her cheeks and her hands came away wet. She wasn't sure if the tears were from laughing or shock. "I think I've gone insane."

Rin smiled at her. A subdued smile—not like the lightning-strike, sun-coming-out-from-behind-clouds smiles of earlier.

A sudden impulse seized her, and she reached out to rest her palm against his cheek. His skin was warm, with just a hint of stubble pricking against her hand.

"You're real," Lily said.

"I am."

"And you're an alien?"

He sighed, then nodded. "And you're not supposed to know that."

"I can imagine." Suddenly aware of her hand resting on his cheek—and how close their faces were to each other's—she pulled back, leaning away from him.

"Let me help you." Rin stood, then offered his hand.

Lily stared at it for a moment, looking for any difference that would set him apart. Webbing between his fingers, stripes or spots or scales.

The only odd thing about his hand was how perfect it was.

Lily shook herself. This was no time to start mooning over some guy. Some hot doctor guy. Who was also an alien.

Oh my God. He's an alien.

"I don't bite, either," Rin said. "In case that's a...very disturbing reassurance that Earthlings need."

She laughed again, but this time, it didn't make her feel unhinged. She took his hand and let him help her to her feet.

Nana's laughter echoed from the house, along with a chittering sound that must be Cyan. The new yoga buddy. Who was also a lizard lady. From the Vega system.

Vegan.

"I get it now." Lily shook her head. "I still can't believe this."

But the evidence was right there. She was holding hands with it, staring into his eyes.

Nana hadn't been delusional after all. Aliens were real.

Chapter Four

Rin tried to keep his focus on his mission, despite the myriad distractions all around him. The beautiful Earthling staring up at him wasn't making it easy.

She had golden hair that was held up in a messy ponytail. Her skin was tanned from the sun and her eyes were a stunning blue. She wore a pale pink T-shirt with a V neck and cut-off denim shorts. Her legs were long, with curves that made her look soft and...

He cleared his throat and glanced at the house. "You know, I bet it's cooler inside."

"What?" She blinked a few times, then seemed to come to her senses. "Oh, right. Of course."

She dropped his hand and stepped back, wiping her palms on the back of her shorts. Perspiration was beading on her chest. He watched a drop trickle down between her breasts.

Rin needed an objective. Something to harness his thoughts.

He remembered Cyan tucking a small satchel into the seat between them in the car before they left. She hadn't been able to grab it earlier.

"Hold on a second." He trotted to the still-open driver's side door, then reached in and picked up the bag. A small cylinder fell from it. When he picked it up, it made a rattling sound.

He turned it over in his hands, walking back toward Lily after kicking the door to the car shut. The cylinder had strange drawings on it that vaguely resembled the creature that Cyan had saved. "Freddie."

"I wonder what this is," he mumbled to himself, shaking the cylinder to make more of the rattling.

Lily was standing near the house, and when she heard the sound, she turned toward him, her eyes wide.

"Don't shake that!" she yelled.

Rin froze. Why the hell shouldn't he shake the cylinder? It couldn't be some sort of bomb, could it? From Lily's reaction, he wasn't sure.

"Oh, crap," Lily said.

He didn't know what was upsetting her until the first of the creatures came shooting out of the house, making horrible yowling noises. It was followed by a dozen more. They bolted right for him.

Nana had told him that *Lily* wouldn't bite, but what about these screaming beasts?

He turned and ran.

Only then did he realize that Cyan's bag was filled with the cylinders.

The rattling noise intensified with his movement, but he didn't dare slow down.

"Don't run!" Lily let out an exasperated sound.

More of the furred beasts appeared from the foliage surrounding them—from under the vehicles and from the back of the house. Climbing wasn't an option for escape. He'd seen how agile Freddie was when climbing the tree.

"How many of these things are there?" he yelled, dodging a couple of brown and black striped creatures. They swiped at his legs as he passed, revealing curved, needle-sharp claws. "Holy shit! What are these?"

"Drop the cans and run," Lily said.

"You just told me *not* to run!"

No matter what she said, Rin wasn't about to stop. Not with these things chasing him.

"Drop the cans and *then* run!"

A gray-furred beast leapt on him, digging its claws into his leg and using them to climb up his body.

"Shit!" he yelled.

Pain stung its way along his nerves as he spun in circles, trying to dislodge it. Another latched onto him, joining the first in its climb, and adding to Rin's agony.

If he tripped and fell, with so many of them in pursuit... They would eat him alive.

The thought was enough to keep him moving, even with the beasts attached to his leg. And his back. Damn, they could climb quickly! Their claws tore at his clothing, digging into his flesh.

"Rin, stop," Lily yelled.

"There is no fucking way I'm stopping."

One of her instructions finally registered, and he chucked the cylinder he was holding as far away as he could. Half a dozen of the razor-clawed things ran after it. A dozen more kept chasing him, no matter how hard he tried to dodge. Another leapt and managed to latch on to this cargo shorts, its claws scoring searing lines down his thigh and calf.

He wanted to kick them or swat them away, but Cyan... Shit, Cyan *liked* these things.

He couldn't hurt them, even if they seemed determined to hurt him.

"Drop the bag," Lily yelled.

Rin had forgotten he was holding it. He dropped it, then bolted away from the house. He wouldn't lead these monsters toward the others.

Something appeared in his path. Something green. No, *someone* green. Cyan.

"Stop," Cyan said.

He skidded to a halt, sand spraying up from his boots as his feet dug furrows into the ground. It was either that, or risk trampling Cyan.

The thing on his back jumped off as soon as he stopped. Cyan stepped forward and gently plucked off one of the wretched skeelbats still clinging to his legs, whispering soft words to it as she did. Someone else was detaching the last one. Lily.

"I'm so sorry," Lily said. "They go crazy for those treats. Nana has them trained to come when she shakes the cans, but she normally has plates ready for them so they head right for the food. Most of them started out as feral strays with no one to care for them. They don't have the best manners toward people."

Rin was shaking from adrenaline and pain. He glanced down to see lines of red crisscrossing his legs. The wounds looked shallow for the most part, but there were dozens of them.

"What are those little monsters?" he said.

"They are not monsters." Cyan snorted an indignant breath from her nostrils, setting the thing on the ground gently. "They are indigenous life forms who have evolved to be companion creatures."

"In what fucked up world are these companion creatures?" Rin said.

"Companion creatures?" Lily said. "We just call them 'pets'."

"Why?" Rin looked genuinely confused.

"I don't know," she said. "Because we pet them?"

"These specific life forms are called 'cats'." Cyan ducked her head, and said, "And I am sorry they hurt you."

How could he stay mad when she looked so upset?

He was still surrounded by those little hellspawn

creatures. *Cats.* He should have brought a stasis field generator. Or a disintegration pistol.

The wounds they'd inflicted on him were starting to burn.

"They aren't venomous, are they?" Rin asked.

Nana had reached them, and she let out a short laugh. "Venomous cats? Now that would be a thing to make you shudder."

Lily glared at Nana, and said, "Cats aren't venomous. But they do have a lot of bacteria in their mouths and on their claws. I don't think any of them bit you, but we should wash out those scratches as soon as we can."

'We'?

His mind provided a tantalizing image of Lily's hands on his legs, using the water and soap cleansing techniques popular on Earth. The thought sent a jolt through him, surprising in its intensity. His skin beaded into goosebumps and his dick actually twitched. He needed to rein himself in quickly.

"No need," he said. "Cyan can use the med-tech functions in her exosuit to heal the wounds and disinfect them."

"I…can not," Cyan said.

It took him a moment to process what she'd said, he was so surprised. "Why not?"

Cyan started wringing her hands again as she explained. "The sensors in my exosuit will create an entry for the life forms that created the wounds, along with an analysis of the extent of the injuries."

"Why is that a problem?" Lily blinked a few times, as if she was still adjusting to the fact that she was speaking to a sentient who was obviously so alien from her experience.

"Cats are companion creatures," Cyan said. "They are rarely found far from human habitations."

Rin understood her predicament at once, and why she'd been so hesitant to approach him for help. Cyan had made contact with an Earthling without clearance.

Even as someone who could pass as human, Rin was under orders to keep contact with Earthlings to a minimum. Cyan was obviously an intelligent alien life form. Contact with Earthlings was absolutely forbidden.

Apparently, his fellow Sadirian soldiers weren't the only ones being affected by the Earth's occupants. He still couldn't believe that so many on the team had actually fallen in love with Earthlings and formed pair-bonds. Rin had interacted with several Earthlings, but none of them had affected him strongly.

He glanced over at Lily. Well, not until today.

He brought himself back to the problem at hand. Helping his friend.

"We can tell them I ran into town to get provisions and encountered them," Rin said.

Cyan shook her head. "The symptoms I am having began with my first exposure to cats. I am afraid that my exosuit will correlate the biological contaminants in my system with those found in your injuries. My activities here will be discovered."

"What's so bad about you hanging out with a bunch of cats?" Lily asked.

"I… I am not supposed to be here." Cyan's spines flattened against her head and all down her back. She bowed her head, and said, "If my activities are discovered, you will all receive mind-wipes and I will be forbidden from returning. I may even be restricted to the Life Ship. I will never see Lillian or her glaring again. They will forget that I even existed."

"Glaring?" Rin asked. Why would Cyan want to see someone glare at her?

"It's another name for a group of cats," Lily said.

"O…kay," he said. "And who is Lillian?"

"That's me," Nana said. "Everybody but Cyan just calls me 'Nana', though."

"Does anything or anyone on this planet have a single, straightforward name?" Rin asked.

"I'm just Lily." Lily half-shrugged and smiled at him. Her cheeks turned pink and she looked away.

"What's a mind-wipe?" Nana asked, bringing him back to task.

"They will erase your memories of me." Cyan's voice was higher than he'd ever heard it. "It will be as though we never met."

"To hell with that," Nana said.

Lily put her hands on her hips and glared at Rin. "No one is erasing our memories."

"It's not up to me," Rin said.

Cyan covered her face and started making a hiss-hiss-hiccup noise. He was pretty sure she was crying.

"Cyan…" He shook his head, not knowing what to say.

"Are you compatible with humans?" Lily asked.

Rin and Nana turned to stare at her.

"I mean…you look human." The blush in Lily's cheeks deepened. "Is your body human-like?"

"Earthlings and Sadirians are closely related." He didn't want to go into the whole "Earth is a lost colony" thing. Lily was dealing with enough as it was.

"Okay, I'm still not sure this isn't all just some sort of intense, late-night pizza related dream," Lily said. "But why don't you just heal normally? I've been scratched up way worse than that."

Cyan dropped her hands to her sides and shook her head. "No, I could not ask that of my friend. He was injured trying to help me, and I am repaying him with selfishness."

"It's not selfishness." Rin spoke more harshly than he'd intended. He softened his voice as he said, "I get it, Cyan. I really do."

"But your injuries—" she said.

Nana cut in. "They're nothing. A couple of days, and he'll be right as rain."

"I do not understand," Cyan said. "How can rain be correct or incorrect?"

Both the Earthlings laughed.

"It's just an expression." Lily cast a reserved smile at him. "But you really will be fine."

"You hear that?" Rin said. "I'll be fine."

Cyan narrowed her gold eyes at him. The huge orange cat she called "Freddie" approached and started walking around her in circles, its tail clinging to her in an odd, almost prehensile fashion. She looked down at him with a forlorn expression.

Rin hit on a way to reassure her. Maybe. "Now that I'm thinking about it, this is going to be great. I don't know of anyone who's let their body heal from any kind of injury without our med-tech. We can observe the process and make notes."

"It'll be a great cover story, too," Lily said. "If anyone asks, you can tell them you were a little too curious about the local wildlife, and then decided to see what it's like for us humans when we pay for our mistakes."

Rin had a sudden urge to hug Lily and thank her. But that would undo the progress he could see that they'd made in convincing Cyan to follow their plan.

"'Us humans'." Lily shook her head. "I can't believe I just said that."

Rin turned back to Cyan. "I can heal on my own. We don't need to use anything that will leave a trail back here.

No one else has to know. That is why you came to me, right?"

"It is, but…" Cyan picked up Freddie and buried her snout in his fur. "Are you certain you will be as correct as rain?"

Rin chuckled. "Yeah."

Cyan's eyes crinkled up and her head tilted back. She let out another huge sneeze, her scales turning orange and white in a pattern that matched the cat.

"Okay, what is up with that?" Lily asked. "Are you allergic to cats or something?"

Cyan sniffed a few times. "What is 'allergic'?"

"You know…" Lily said. "When certain things make you sneeze? Like people who are allergic to cats. I guess their bodies don't know quite how to react to their…fur or something, and being around cats makes them sneeze or cough or get itchy. I'm not a doctor and I've never really studied them before."

A reaction of that sort would be unheard of on the ships and in the dome worlds of the Coalition. Everything was too controlled. The air was constantly purified, and the food held only the molecules needed to sustain life.

Cyan perked up, a huge smile splitting her face. "Does it make their coloration change?"

"Not…humans." Lily glanced over at Rin, as if seeking support. He wasn't quite sure what to say. "With mild allergies, they usually just make people sneeze and stuff."

This could explain Cyan's issue. And if it wasn't dangerous, then her problem was mostly solved. If he could deal with scratches, he was sure Cyan could deal with the discomfort of her sneezing fits—especially when he saw how lovingly she cradled the cat in her arms.

"Are allergies dangerous?" he asked.

"Well, some allergies can be dangerous. I don't know about the sneezing kind. Like I said, I'm not a doctor or anything." Lily gestured toward Cyan. "And she's a lizard person, so I don't even know how this all applies."

"She's a Vegan," Nana said. "Cyan's from the Vega system."

Lily looked up at the sky and took a deep breath, then let it out slowly. "This can't be real."

"It can and it is." Nana turned and started toward the house. "Now let's go inside and sort this out. Starting with washing out those scratches."

"Right." Lily gestured toward the house. "Come on. I'll help you."

"Thanks," he said.

Inside the house, there was a couch to the right of the door in an inviting seating area with a few chairs and a bookshelf. Some yoga mats were propped up in the corner.

He thought of the yoga classes Sarah taught for the members of the Department of Homeworld Security stationed in Florida. She'd probably get along great with Nana.

Nana.

The title was familial. Using it caused a warmth to spread through his chest. Or maybe it was thinking about how he was happy he could help his friend.

Or the cats really could be venomous.

He needed to learn more about the creatures.

Cyan sat on the couch and Nana settled into a chair nearby. Several cats had followed them inside, including the one with orange and white stripes. It jumped up on the couch next to Cyan and started emitting a low, rumbling sound again.

"What the hell is that noise?" Rin asked.

Cyan wrapped her arms around the cat and hugged it against her chest. "It is called 'purring' and it means he is happy." She buried her snout in the cat's fur again. "I am happy to see you, too, Freddie."

She pulled back and gently touched her nose to the cat's, who sniffed her, and then rubbed his face against her chin. Cyan's lips stretched in a huge smile as she stroked the cat's back.

"If you *are* allergic to cats, you should consider maybe not rubbing your face on them," Lily said. "And maybe wash your face and hands after touching them, to get the allergens off."

"But he is soft and snuggly," Cyan said.

Lily's eyebrows lifted. She shook her head.

"How is that so cute?" she murmured.

Rin chuckled. The stinging in his legs was turning into dull throbs. He pushed the pain aside, keeping his focus on making sure Cyan was indeed safe with her new *friends*.

"Tell me again how long you've been having these reactions to Freddie and the others," Rin said.

"It started a few days after I discovered Freddie in the woods and followed him here," Cyan said. "I do not know what changed, but suddenly I would have fits of sneezing. After a while, my coloration began to alter as well."

Nana made a tsking noise. "It really does sound like an allergy. I can't believe I didn't think of that before. It's almost like I never read *War of the Worlds*."

Lily took a sudden step forward. "You don't think—"

"Oh, sweet pea, it was only a joke." Nana let out a laugh. "Our bacteria and illnesses can't hurt Cyan."

Cyan nodded. "All of us have been inoculated against Earth-born pathogens and also checked thoroughly to ensure we are not carrying any harmful pathogens ourselves."

"Well, that's good," Lily said.

Rin smiled at the Earthling who had just moments ago firmly believed that aliens couldn't possibly exist, and now was showing concern for one she'd only just met. She glared at him when she met his gaze.

"What?" she asked.

He shook his head. "The human capacity for empathy and compassion will never cease to amaze me."

Lily's lips parted, and for a moment, all he could think about was how soft they appeared. Her cheeks turned red and she looked away, clamping her mouth shut.

Cyan let out another sneeze.

Chapter Five

There were aliens hanging out in Nana's house. Real, live aliens. Cute ones, too.

The way Cyan kept burying her nose in Freddie's fur made Lily want to say, "Aww." She kept it under wraps, not wanting to start an interstellar incident by accidentally offending anyone.

The cat looked like it weighed about as much as the lizard person—*Vegan*—but he seemed to be cautious in how he was lying next to her, glancing up at Cyan's face when he shifted positions. It was almost as if he was checking on her, or feeling protective, like Rin obviously did.

Which brought Lily to the other cute alien in the room. Although, "cute" wasn't a strong enough word.

Handsome, rugged, masculine, gorgeous. Any of those would work.

Rin looked like he'd just stepped off the cover of a romance novel. His shirt kept straining against the muscles of his back as he inspected Cyan, occasionally consulting the high-tech watch that seemed to be feeding him information.

As if his looks weren't enough, he was considerate, well-spoken, and had given Lily the best compliment she had ever received in her life. That comment about her impressing him with compassion...

She was heading into deep water where this guy was concerned, and without a life jacket. Worse—without an action plan.

"Lily. Lily!" Nana's voice broke through Lily's thoughts.

"What?"

Nana smirked and shook her head. "It looks like we're going to have company for a while. I'm going to go prep the guest room for Rin. You can have my room. Get the cot out of the closet and set it up here so Cyan and I can camp out together, okay?"

"Wait, what?" Lily asked.

"I'm not risking a mind-wipe because someone notices the scratches on Rin's legs," Nana said. "They're staying here for a couple of days."

Lily had really zoned out to miss all that. It had to be from the shock of finding out that aliens were real. Rin couldn't be *that* distracting.

"I don't want to inconvenience you," Rin said.

"The cot won't carry your weight," Nana said.

"I meant about staying—"

Nana turned to Cyan, cutting Rin off. "How long did

you tell them you'd be gone this time?"

"Several days," Cyan said.

"Then I'm not sending you back with Rin all scratched up when there's talk of 'mind-wipes' and 'being forbidden' from doing something you love." Nana let out a derisive snort.

"Well, you don't have to give up your room," Rin said.

"I'm aware." Nana headed down the hall toward the guest room.

"You'll never win." Lily shook her head as she opened the door to the small closet just off the living room. "When she's like this, she always gets her way."

Lily dragged the cot over to the couch and propped it up against one of the overstuffed chairs next to it. She started pushing the coffee table away, and Rin leaned into it to help her, then rose as she moved to rearrange the chairs.

"Is she like this often?" he asked.

"Stubborn as a mule?" Lily laughed. "Yeah. You get used to it, though."

"I have not yet encountered a mule," Cyan said. "I would like to do so someday."

Lily snorted. "If you get along this well with Nana, you'll probably love them."

"I can hear you, you know," Nana shouted.

Lily started setting up the cot. "Ears like a bat," she murmured.

"I *have* encountered those," Cyan said. "They are

fascinating creatures. The diversity within their kind is truly staggering."

Cyan kept going on, peppering them with statistics and factoids about bats that Lily only half paid attention to. Okay, less than half. She was more focused on getting the cot set up and dealing with the reality of aliens in her Nana's living room.

And trying to ignore Rin's proximity.

"One of their food sources is gnats," Cyan said. "It intrigues me that those words are so similar, but I have not been able to determine if there is a causal relation to the naming conventions among humans who use this language. I have spoken with Magenta, our chief linguistics expert, and she is looking into the possibilities."

"Let me guess," Lily said. "Her stripes are magenta colored?"

Cyan let out a series of little snorts that sounded like a chuckle. "Indeed. Our Vegan names are unpronounceable by human or Sadirian palates, and Sarah had already named several of us based on our stripe colors before we established a dialogue. As the Protector of our people and the chief liaison between Vegans and Earthlings, we have decided to continue this tradition."

"Wait, Sarah as in 'The Old Oak' restaurant Sarah?" Lily asked.

"Yes." Cyan beamed. "I am one of the lucky Vegans who is honored to live with her in her tree home. It is lovely."

"Wow." Lily shook her head. "It really is a small world."

"Earth is an excellent size," Cyan said. "We are so grateful to have found a new world for our people that can accommodate us without putting an undue burden on your ecosystems."

"Wait, for like...all of you?" Lily asked.

Rin was standing by the couch behind Cyan. He caught Lily's eye and shook his head vigorously, then cast a concerned look at Cyan. The Vegan was quiet for a moment, staring intently at Freddie.

After the constant stream of sound, her silence made Lily's stomach clench. Had Lily said something wrong?

Lily fished for something to take the conversation to safer terrain. "I didn't think there were that many different colors. How can there be enough names for an entire species?"

Rin's mouth dropped open briefly and he covered his eyes.

Apparently, her new topic wasn't safe after all.

"There are quite a few Earth words for different colors," Cyan said. Her voice was subdued. "Especially since we are using all languages. Even Vegans who share a stripe color will have individual names."

"You don't all have to have different names," Lily said. "There are lots of humans who share the same one. Like me and my Nana."

Cyan smiled at her, but didn't say more. Lily didn't know why this was a sensitive topic, but wanted to help her feel better.

"You know what else rhymes with 'bat'?" Lily winked as she said, "'Cat'."

Rin nodded his approval, but still cast a concerned look at Cyan. He visibly relaxed when she smiled.

Cyan's laugh came out as a series of hisses. "It does, indeed." She gripped Freddie's face and rubbed their noses together, saying, "Cats are amazing creatures. Detached, yet affectionate."

"Are Vegans not...huggy?" Lily asked.

Rin started to laugh, but turned it into a cough. The smile he cast at Lily made her toes curl.

"Most Vegans are more reserved, I would say," Cyan said.

"Well, if you ever want a hug, just ask." Rin patted Cyan's shoulder and she smiled up at him.

It was such a sweet scene. Most of the scifi movies Lily had seen portrayed aliens as monstrous creatures. Cyan and Rin didn't seem scary at all. Lily *liked* them.

Rin turned toward one of the chairs and winced, pulling at his pantlegs. Lily glanced down and saw blood seeping through the fabric.

"I'm so sorry," Lily said. "I was supposed to help with that."

"I can assist." Cyan leaned forward, but couldn't seem

to dislodge Freddie's weight across her lap.

"That's okay." Lily cringed at the eagerness she could hear in her own voice. "I can take care of it. You spend time with Freddie."

Cyan settled back onto the couch with a contented smile. Nana crossed the room, heading for the kitchen to make lunch, probably.

"What are you still standing around for?" Nana hooked her thumb toward the hallway. "Take him to the bathroom before those really start to sting."

"Cats can sting people?" Cyan's golden eyes were wide.

Nana laughed. "No, sweetie. Just sit back and I'll explain."

Without really thinking about it, Lily hooked her arm in Rin's elbow. His eyes widened, but then he smiled at her. Well, smirked, more like.

Lily put on her best scowl as she led him from the room. "You heard Nana. Let's get you cleaned up."

Chapter Six

Lily led Rin to a small bathroom and closed the door, muffling the conversation in the other room.

"I hope it's okay that I'm helping with this," she said. "I just need a little bit of space and I have a feeling this is the best I'm going to get for a while."

"It's fine. And I can take care of myself."

"Really?" She crossed her arms, cocking her hip to the side as she stared at him. "What did you have in mind?"

"I haven't had a chance to think about it yet. I've been focused on Cyan. I guess I'd start with a scan?"

"All you'll find is bacteria." Her lips pulled into a frown, deep furrows appearing between her eyebrows. "You're sure you guys have immunity to Earth's pathogens, right? I mean, there are a lot of them."

He laughed. "I'm sure."

"Okay." After a pause, she added, "Wow, that must be nice."

She leaned over and started untying her shoes. There wasn't much room for two people in the small space, and her movements kept her close to him in areas…he hadn't let anyone close to in a long time.

"What are you doing?" he asked.

"Prepping to get in the tub." She pointed at his feet. "You should take off your boots and socks."

"O...kay."

If he tried to lean over to untie his boots, they would bump into each other. He ended up sitting on the edge of the bathtub. By the time his feet were bare, Lily was standing again, staring at him. Her gaze was shuttered, leaving him wondering what she was thinking about.

There were so many things she must be processing. Aliens, "lizard people", advanced technology. But she was staring at his legs. If he had to guess, she was focused on helping him, just as he did with his patients. Even with everything else going on.

His chest felt tight at the thought. He looked away, but then his attention became caught on the soft skin covering her perfectly smooth legs. He didn't get to stare at them as long as he wanted, because she dropped to her knees in front of him.

Fantasies played in his head. Images he should not indulge filled his mind.

Lily leaned forward and started gently rolling up the cuffs of his cargo shorts. Of course, that's all she'd been planning to do. He chided himself for the pang of disappointment he felt.

Just because several of his colleagues had hit it off with

Earthlings right away didn't mean that he would as well. From what he knew, it was an oddity even by Earth standards that some of them had bonded so quickly. He couldn't deny that he felt drawn to Lily, but that didn't mean she felt the same way.

"Oh, wow, they really did get you good." She glanced up at him, concerned etched in her features. "Not that it's good what they did. It's just an Earth expression—"

"Don't worry about it. I'm good with Earth idioms." He smiled and dared to reach out and put his hand on her shoulder. "I appreciate your help."

Her eyes widened and she opened her mouth to draw in a deep breath. For a moment, he wondered if maybe she *was* feeling something toward him. He shouldn't let himself dream.

She pinched her mouth into a thin line, then stood. "Turn around and put your feet in the tub. Please," she added.

"Yes, Doctor."

She let out a puff of breath and rolled her eyes, just the reaction he'd hoped for. A small smile followed as she relaxed a bit. She stepped into the tub after he'd situated himself, then started up the water.

As she moved, her shirt shifted from side to side, giving him a clear view of her small breasts. He tilted his head up so he was staring at the ceiling, but not before catching a tantalizing glimpse of her dusky nipples.

"What are you doing?" she said. "You're going to fall

over backward and hit your head on something."

"I understand that nudity is a social taboo in your culture." He was glad the water was loud enough to mask their conversation from the room outside. Cyan and Nana would probably wonder what the hell was going on otherwise.

"I guess so," Lily said. "I've never thought about it."

"Your shirt is a little loose."

"Great. Of course it is." She sighed, then said, "You're a doctor. I'm sure it's nothing you haven't seen before."

"I'm a field medic, actually." He turned his head back toward her, keeping his eyes shut. "And nudity isn't a big deal where I'm from. We don't have much in the way of privacy."

"That sounds awful."

"When it's all you've known, it doesn't bother you." In theory, anyway.

Rin had always longed for more than a bunk and storage locker, especially knowing that nothing he had actually belonged to him. He didn't even own his time.

Soldiers assigned to combat duties or ship operations had designated rest periods and could earn resources. They could build a life outside the fleet.

Medical personnel... Well, they were valued about as much as the people sent in to be patched up on the regen beds. He'd never heard of one retiring.

He heard the pitch of the water change as Lily must have

put something in the stream. Cold water hit his legs. He yelped, jerking his feet away, which threw him off balance.

He started to fall backwards, arms flailing as he tried to find anything to grab onto. Time seemed to slow.

He opened his eyes just in time to see Lily grab his shirt and pull him toward her. The hem made a ripping noise, but she managed to slow his fall enough that he could reach behind himself and slam his hand on the floor, further reducing his speed.

Lily wasn't satisfied, though. With a determined gleam in her eyes, she grabbed his shoulders. She was a fraction of his weight, but she hung on as if she really thought she could stop his descent.

She ended up falling with him. He landed with a loud thud, but at least he managed to distribute the impact across his back.

Lily landed on top of him.

Their chests were plastered together, her cheek against his. Strands of her hair tickled his nose.

"Crap," she said. "Are you all right?"

He was better than all right. His body reacted to her proximity faster than he would have believed possible. His dick reached maximum capacity just as she brought her knees to either side of his torso, pushing herself upright and resting her pelvis flat against his crotch.

Her eyes widened and she gasped. Both of them froze, staring at each other, breath coming quick as their chests worked to bring their bodies air that suddenly didn't seem to hold enough oxygen. Pleasure streaked through him, flying along his nerves and heating him more than the midday sun.

"Lily—"

Before he could finish his thought, the door to the bathroom opened. It missed whacking Rin in the head by about a centimeter.

"What the hell are you two doing in here?" Nana stood in the doorway, staring at the shower. Her gaze dropped down, her eyebrows hitching when she saw them on the floor, then a huge grin split her face.

"About damned time," Nana said. "And you sure picked a looker."

"Nana!" Lily yelled.

"Go on and get you some." Nana laughed, pulling the door shut just as Lily threw a box of tissues that had been sitting on the back of the toilet. It bounced off the door and landed on Rin's forehead.

"They're going to be a while," Nana said, raising her voice loud enough for them to hear her over the water.

Rin rubbed his temple where the box had hit him.

"Sorry…" Lily leaned forward and gently touched the spot.

That didn't bother him nearly as much as the way she had squirmed while reaching out to grab the box in the first place, and then settled right back on that perfect resting spot when she was done.

Well, "bother" wasn't the right word.

"It's okay," he said.

Really okay.

He kept the last thought to himself.

Chapter Seven

Lily was not going to have sex with an alien on the floor of her Nana's bathroom. It wasn't happening. No matter how tempting it was.

How can it be so tempting?

Maybe part of it was that she could feel his erection against her in exactly the right place. Her body lit up like kindling touched by a match.

Goosebumps raced along her skin. Her mouth went dry, her chest felt tight. She wanted more than anything to lean forward and kiss him.

But she wasn't adventurous. She wasn't daring and reckless. And she sure as hell cared that there were two people right outside who knew—or thought they knew—what she was doing in here with Rin.

Yes, she wanted to be more spontaneous. But she definitely was not comfortable with…any of this. Whatever it was.

Emotionally, anyway. Physically… That was another matter entirely.

Her nerve endings were practically having a meltdown.

She could feel heat and wetness between her legs, an aching need clenching her core that she hadn't felt in way too long. She wasn't sure she'd ever felt anything quite like Rin's effect on her.

And there was Rin, still lying under her, staring at her with those fathomless dark eyes.

She licked her lips and his gaze followed the movement.

Not helping.

"Is your head okay?" she said.

"Which one?" He grinned up at her for a moment, then cleared his throat when she only scowled back at him. "I understand in your Earth vernacular there are two."

"Yes, yes. I get it."

"I'm fine," he said. "I think."

"You're not sure?"

"Well, you're welcome to inspect me."

She frowned at him, but still couldn't seem to convince her legs to move. For one thing, it would create more of that delicious friction that seemed to short-circuit her rational thought. And worse, it would bring this moment to an end.

"I'm sorry," he said. "I didn't mean to offend you. I'm just not used to reacting like this to someone. I didn't even know my body was capable of it."

"What?" Her throat felt like it was collapsing on itself. The word came out as a squeak. She coughed, then said, "You didn't know you could...you know."

His brow furrowed briefly, but then he laughed, his straight teeth gleaming in the light from the high window behind them. "I knew I could get an erection. I didn't know it was possible to get one so quickly without *Coupling*."

Confusion—and a hefty dose of curiosity—overcame her shyness. "How would you couple without getting an erection?"

"Not 'couple'. *Coupling*. It's a drug my people use to control intercourse."

"Like birth control?"

"That's among its functions." He sneered as he spoke. Whatever this drug was, he didn't appear to be a fan. "It takes the body through all the stages of arousal through climax, with or without a partner."

"That sounds…really boring."

He laughed and she felt a smile tug at her lips in response.

"I've always thought so," he said.

"I guess there's something to be said for doing things low-tech. It's bound to be more…compelling."

When he spoke, his voice had a rasp to it that again made her toes want to curl. "*You* are compelling."

"That's just gravity," she said. "And biology."

She started to rise, but he rested his hands lightly on her hips, urging her to stay in place. It didn't take much to convince her. Most of her willpower was tied up in not grinding against him. That little bit of added pressure sent tingling sparks dancing along her nerves.

She watched his throat move as he swallowed.

"It isn't gravity," he said. "I believe the term you use is 'chemistry'. At least, that's my experience of our interactions."

She was about to argue, but paused. "Wait. Interactions?" She emphasized the 'S' at the end.

Sure, what they had going on at the moment was absolutely atomic, and she'd been drawn to him from the moment she laid eyes on him. But he was talking like she had caught his interest even before she landed on him. They'd only just met, and she couldn't remember doing anything…memorable.

"I've never met someone who draws me in the way you do," he said.

She let out a snort, finally finding the will to rise. "Maybe you should scan yourself. I think you may have hit your head when you fell."

"I don't need a scan." He pushed himself up onto his elbows.

"There must not be a lot of women where you're from." She murmured the words under her breath, but he heard her, even over the sound of the water still filling the tub.

"Half of our population is female. What does that have to do with anything?"

He rose to his feet a bit awkwardly in the tiny space. His chest brushed against her arms, his heat radiated toward her. She retreated into the tub, but he followed, sitting back on the edge as he had before.

Rather than answer, she knelt down and started splashing water onto his legs. He didn't bother trying to look away anymore. From the corner of her eye, she could see he was staring at her face instead of her cleavage.

Moment over, then.

"Are you considered unattractive among Earthlings?" he asked.

"Wow." She felt her eyes widen at the bold question, but pulled herself together, grabbing the soap and lathering her hands. "I'm okay."

As she began cleaning his wounds, he said, "If you're only considered moderately attractive, I'm not the one who needs a cranial scan."

She snorted and said, "Smooth."

"Really? I figured my legs would feel rough to you. Especially when compared with your own."

She bit back her retort when she saw the earnestness of his gaze. For a moment, she'd forgotten he was from another planet.

Shaking her head, she said, "I was talking about your words."

"I *have* adapted to Earth language and communication better than my peers. This conversation is still a little confusing."

"I just think you're laying it on a little thick." Dang, she was going to have to watch out for using idioms with him. "It seems like you're trying to make me like you, with all the compliments and 'chemistry' talk."

"I've meant everything I said."

She didn't know how to respond to that, so she focused on cleaning out his wounds and rinsing them. It probably stung like crazy, but he didn't complain.

When she was done, she stopped the water and pulled out the drain plug. She grabbed a towel and patted his legs dry as gently as she could.

"It makes it hard to trust, doesn't it?" he said.

"What does?"

"Betrayal."

Her heart seemed to clench at the word—at how much he'd gleaned from her in their brief time together. She shrugged, trying to act like it was no big deal.

"Everybody has an agenda," she said.

"That's true."

She was surprised he didn't try to refute her statement. At least he was being honest about that.

"What's yours?" he asked.

"Excuse me?"

"You're someone. You have to have an agenda, too. Something you want to have or do. Something you want to make of your life."

Crap. He had her there.

"I want to help people." The words tumbled out before

she could stop them. Worse, once they started, they kept coming. "My family owns an import/export company. Nana mostly trades in weird, exotic merchandise. I want to use our contacts and facilities to start shifting resources to where they're most needed. Clean water for people living in deserts. Food, clothing. And the means for people to create more of what they need so they aren't reliant on others and can truly thrive where they are."

"Wow." He smiled up at her. "That's quite an agenda."

She shrugged. "What about you?"

"I want to help Cyan keep her secrets," he said. "Our government is…" His lips pulled down in a grimace. "Let's just say that their agenda and mine are quite at odds."

"I can see where you'd want to distance yourself from people who drug their citizens instead of just letting them have sex."

"They don't let us have anything." He practically spat the words. "Not even real emotions. Everything is managed with *Balance* or *Coupling* or worse."

Her blood chilled. She couldn't imagine living among people whose emotions had been taken from them or twisted and controlled.

"You seem to have pretty strong feelings on he matter," she said.

He shook his head, then smirked again. "The drugs they use to regulate emotions don't work on me. Something in my DNA blocks them."

"And yet they let you run around on your own? As controlling as you make them sound, that surprises me."

He shrugged. "What they don't know can't hurt me."

"But you just told me."

"I trust you."

"Why?"

"I'm not sure," he said. "I guess because it feels right."

Chapter Eight

Part of Rin wondered if he'd gone completely insane. From the look on Lily's face, she was thinking the same thing.

She was right to find it strange that he was trusting her with so much so quickly. But he hadn't felt any kind of connection to someone in so long. It had never been as strong as this, either.

True, there weren't many people she could tell these specific secrets to, but it could land him in some very uncomfortable situations if the wrong people found out about his unusual immunity. More Sadirians would be roaming Earth soon.

He pushed away thoughts of the *Reckoning*'s arrival. They still had a little time to prepare.

Lily helped distract him with more questions.

"What about *Coupling?*" she asked.

"What about it?"

"Does it work on you?"

He laughed. "No, it doesn't."

"So when you had sex before, your partners were

drugged, but you weren't."

With what he knew of her culture, he could see where that would trouble her. She didn't seem like the kind of person who would tolerate any kind of power disparity well, especially during such an intimate interaction.

"I always told them before we started anything," he said.

"Oh." Her shoulders slumped. She actually looked disappointed.

He didn't understand her reaction. Unless she was feeling a connection to him as well. She *had* taken her time extricating herself from their extremely comfortable predicament earlier.

Sharing this part of himself was no small matter for him. It meant something. And if it meant something to her, too, he could understand her disappointment at the thought of him telling another.

"Not about my immunity," he said. "I told them I was one of the few weirdos in our society who didn't want to use *Coupling* during sex. There aren't many, but it does happen."

Her gaze returned to his and she smiled.

The connection was real. It couldn't be his imagination.

"And that makes you weird?" she asked.

"It's kind of like someone having a kink on Earth. My last lover was more put off by the emotional component that I experienced than by the physical ones."

He hadn't meant to share that much, but it was out now.

He couldn't even tell himself he regretted it. Sharing this part of himself with Lily felt right.

"I don't understand," she said.

"Clara is part of a group of soldiers who had their emotions completely suppressed. It's supposed to make them more focused in battle. When I told her I had feelings for her, she ended our relationship."

"That's awful."

"The whole experience has made it difficult for me to trust most people." He smirked. "I still don't know what her agenda was, but I'm sure she had one."

Lily shook her head, letting out a somber laugh. "This is all profoundly disturbing."

"I don't mean to trouble you."

"I'd rather know. The fact that you and Cyan are here— along with whoever you don't want learning about her allergies—makes me think Earth isn't just a pit-stop for you guys before you move along to some other place."

"It isn't. Well, not for Cyan and her people, anyway."

He doubted it would be for his people either. The Coalition's interest in Earth only seemed to be growing. Thank the stars the Vegans had arrived and formed an alliance with Earthlings first. Knowing that the species who had created most of the Sadirians' technology had already staked a claim to the planet might give the High Council second thoughts about their usual strong-arm tactics for assimilating new cultures.

Somehow, he didn't think any of that knowledge would reassure Lily.

"Why was Cyan upset when we were talking about there not being many words for her people to use as names if they stick with colors?" Lily said the words gently, as if she sensed the wound that lurked just beneath the surface of the conversation.

He had already shared so much with her. And with Nana and Cyan's friendship, he knew Lily would want to understand.

"The Vegan homeworld was destroyed tens of thousands of years ago," Rin said. "They've been roaming through space on their Life Ship ever since, their population dwindling. There aren't many of them left."

"How could it take them so long to resettle?"

"From what Cyan has shared with me, they wanted to find another race to care for and learn from. It's part of the philosophy they adopted when they left their solar system."

"It's admirable, but…"

He chuckled. "You wonder what *their* agenda is?"

"Kind of."

"Cyan hasn't told me directly, but I think their homeworld's destruction was caused by something they did to it. Their journey has been a kind of penance for that."

"How sad."

"They stopped off at our homeworld, Sadr-4, a few thousand years ago, but I guess we didn't make the cut. Our leaders took the tech the Vegans shared, but then started using it for genetic engineering and to turn trade into conquest."

"And the Vegans didn't put a stop to it?"

"No. I'm not sure why." He shrugged. "They just left instead."

"And now they're settling here." Her eyes widened and the color leached from her face. "Oh no. They aren't going to offer us their technology, are they? Because we're still learning how to deal with our own advancements, and I'm not sure we wouldn't do the same thing—"

"You don't have to worry about the Vegans."

The Coalition was another matter.

"This is a lot to process," she said.

"I know. You're doing an amazing job."

Rin reached out to her and helped her step from the tub. Water splashed on his feet as he did. Once more, they were standing chest-to-chest in the small room.

"Your feet are wet," he said.

"That happens when you've been standing in water." One corner of her mouth twitched up.

"Allow me." He took the towel from her hands and knelt, gently dabbing the water from her calves and feet.

Her legs were perfect. He wanted to run his hands over them, to feel her skin against his, but didn't know how she'd react. Things were happening fast enough between them as it was. Or maybe not fast enough. He didn't know how much time they would actually have together.

"You don't have to do that," she said.

"I know. It only seems polite, after you took such good care of me."

"Do your scratches feel better?" Her voice had a husky quality that made him smile.

"They do, thanks."

He stood and hung the towel over the shower rod, staring down at her. How soft would her lips be against his? How much warmer would she feel pressed against his body when he wasn't lying on a cold tile floor?

"Lily, I—" Before he could finish his thought, his watch beeped at him. "Shit," he said.

"What is it?"

"Someone wanting to check in. I need to get far enough away that they can't see this structure. We left word that we were going out into the woods to survey the wildlife."

Lily reached behind him and opened the door. "Then what are you waiting for? Go."

He wasn't sure what he'd been about to say, but still resented the intrusion. If it was Nika, he would give her a piece of his mind.

He bolted from the bathroom and ran through the living room. As he passed Cyan and Lillian, he said, "Getting a call from base."

Cyan started to sit forward, trying to lift the heavy cat from her lap.

"There's nothing to worry about," Lily said. "Rin will handle it."

Her confidence in him warmed his heart. Now, he just had to live up to it.

He slipped through the back door and sprinted deep into the woods. The soft sand beneath his bare feet slowed him down. He threaded through a patchy spot of grass, hoping the solid vegetable strata would help. Sudden pain pierced his feet in several spots.

"Ow! Shit, shit, shit, shit, shit."

He spun around, hopping on one foot, then the other, until he finally reached sand again. Plopping on the ground, he felt a moment of relief. He looked for what might be causing the pain, and saw half a dozen round spheres embedded in his feet, each about the size of his little finger's nail. They were covered in spikes that bent at the end, creating wicked-looking hooks.

Even the plant life seemed out to get him.

"What the hell is it with this place?"

The beeping of his watch intensified. The house wasn't as far away as he wanted, but it should be out of sight with the thick foliage. Trying to regain control of his breathing, he activated the connection.

"You've reached R-88-b1. How may I help you?" he said.

"Rin?" Ari's face appeared in the tiny screen of the watch, his bald head reflecting the afternoon sun.

Shit.

"Ari?" Rin mimicked Ari's tone and expression, trying to look just as confused to throw Ari off his game. Hopefully.

Ari scowled, his amber skin crinkling around his mouth. "Are you okay?"

"I'm fine. Just a little winded. You ever try to keep up with an enthusiastic Vegan with an exosuit?"

"Actually, I have." Ari shook his head and snorted. "Where's your vehicle?"

"I mistakenly decided to get a little exercise and go for a stroll. This area is fucking hot."

"Don't overdo. You don't have your uniform to protect you from the elements. Remember to hydrate."

"Yes, sir, parental-unit-sir."

Ari snorted again. "And next time you requisition a vehicle, make sure to run it past me first."

"Sorry about that. Cyan was so excited about the field trip. And honestly, how do you say no to her?"

Ari smiled. "She can be hard to resist."

"Speaking of hard to resist, how's our fearless leader's training going?"

"Not so good. Cerulean is trying to help, but Kira just isn't connecting with her exosuit like they expected. It was so natural for Sarah, we thought Kira would have an even easier time with it."

"Is her nanNet interfering?"

"Who knows. Sarah keeps saying that Kira's overthinking it and trying too hard."

"What do you think?"

"Honestly? I think she misses Brendan. I'd like to see her train if he was down here, too."

"Yeah, but he needs to run the main base in Montana."

"Plus he hates the weather here." Ari grinned.

Rin wasn't that fond of it either. Or of the bizarre plant-things that had attached themselves to his feet.

"How long are you and Cyan going to be out there?" Ari asked.

"I'm not sure. A couple of days, at least."

"Days?" Ari's eyebrow muscles furrowed. Part of the glitch in his genetic engineering had made him completely hairless. From the looks he garnered from women during their rare trips into town for supplies, it didn't diminish his attractiveness at all. Sarah sure as hell was a fan.

"Have you noticed how many life forms there are in Florida?" Rin asked. "Lizards and bugs and snakes and cats." Rin shivered at the last, remembering the recent attack.

"Cats?"

Double-shit.

Cats were a companion animal, not the wildlife he and Cyan were supposed to be studying. If Ari realized that, he might figure out that they weren't quite as far into the wilderness as Rin was trying to get everyone to believe.

"Did you see a cat?" Ari pressed.

Rin didn't want to lie to him. What had Lily called the cats when they'd first attacked? The ones with no human caretakers?

"Yeah. It could have been a feral stray." *At one point in its life.*

Rin could see Ari looking around his space, as if checking whether he was alone. Then he leaned closer to his own watch, his cheek and one eye filling Rin's tiny screen.

Ari lowered his voice, and said, "If you see one again, do you think you could capture it for me and bring it back to the base?"

Rin was baffled. "What the hell do you want with a cat?"

"Have you not watched Earth cat videos? Cygnus X, those things are adorable."

"I'll...see what I can do," Rin said.

He couldn't keep from smiling back when a broad grin stretched across Ari's face. Ari had no idea what he was getting into.

"Okay," Ari said. "Check in soon."

"Affirmative."

Rin ended the transmission, shaking his head as he turned to the immediate problem—Earth's very-not-adorable plant life.

Chapter Nine

Lily was getting used to this whole "alien" thing. Sure, there was a lizard lady on her couch, chatting happily with her Nana and petting two of the cats who had joined them. And somewhere in the backyard, there was a gorgeous guy from another planet running around.

A guy Lily had straddled on the floor of the bathroom.

She wanted to do so much more.

If he'd only had sex with people who used that awful-sounding drug, he must have been denied so many things. The sense of connection and fun and…

Who was she kidding? She hadn't felt those things herself yet. With Rin, though… She had a feeling things would be different.

She was already drawn to him. Now that she'd had a few minutes to think, she realized it went beyond physical attraction.

His passion for what he believed in and his desire to help his friend and to take care of others made him that much harder to resist. For the first time in years, Lily was wondering if it would be so bad to give in to temptation.

This was ridiculous. Rin was an alien. What had Nana called him? Satyrian? That wasn't right.

Someone knocked on the door. Lily's heart beat faster. Rin must be back. But why was he knocking?

As she crossed the room, she said, "What kind of alien is Rin again?"

"He is Sadirian," Cyan said, with a particular sibilance Lily was starting to get used to.

"Sadirian." Lily murmured the word. She liked how it sounded.

She was eager to pick up where they'd left off in their earlier conversation. Especially if they could get some privacy.

Opening the door, she felt the broad smile of anticipation on her face, her heart pounding in her chest.

The beat seemed to stutter for a moment. Her mind went blank as it tried to comprehend what was before her.

Ants. Giant ants. Giant ants as tall as Lily, standing on two legs and with enormous heads as big as watermelons and grapefruit-sized segmented eyes and too many arms to count and gleaming cocoa-brown carapaces and—

Lily screamed. A sustained note of pure terror that rang through the trees around them.

In front of her, the two giant ants stepped back, grabbing onto each other and letting out a screech that made Lily's ears ring. Their antennae stiffened like lightning rods on top of their heads and their eyes strobed from white to black and white to black over and over.

Her lungs emptied, Lily finally stopped screaming. She felt dizzy from lack of air, the world spinning around her in a surreal swirl. She could hear scuffling behind her, but didn't want to take her eyes off the *giant ant people* standing right in front of her.

The ants kept on making their terrible sound for moments longer, their many stick-like arms wrapped around each other in a tight embrace. The eyes of the one on Lily's left went completely black and its antennae flattened against its head. It looked up to the sky, letting out a broken chirr that sounded almost like a sob.

"Sister, it is so ugly!" The ant with the darkened eyes spoke in a strange echoing voice, accompanied by chirrs, clicks, and a whirring sound reminiscent of a cricket.

The one on the right started stroking the other's face with her antennae. "Calm yourself, Sister," it—she?—said, in the same strange voice.

The first turned back to stare at Lily, her segmented eyes swirling with pale yellow lights. "It looks like a deformed larva. So pale... And with only those two swollen arms."

"Sister..."

Lily reached into her memory and pulled up what she knew about ant larva.

Okay, she was pale, but she didn't look like a larva. At least Earth ant larva.

But these were ant *people*. They were probably another

kind of alien.

Oh crap.

In a low voice, the first ant said, "And its antennae… They're so thin. Impossibly thin. And there are millions of them. *Millions.*"

"Sister…" the second ant person said.

"Look at its optic organs," the first one whispered. "They're no bigger than scent-vents."

She snorted out of nostrils that were indeed about the size of Lily's eyes.

"Sister!"

The second ant finally seemed to get through to the first. They turned to face each other, loosening their embrace, and the second said, "Your translator unit is active."

"What?" The yellow of the first ant's eyes turned a dull olive green. Her antennae slumped and most of her arms pulled together in front of her chest, kind of like a Praying Mantis.

Lily tried not to think about giant Praying Mantises.

"Oh no… That was unforgivably rude of me." The first ant bowed low. "I didn't mean to offend you. I was so frightened." She shook her head. "That is no excuse. I sincerely apologize for my words, and hope you allow me to make amends."

The second ant's eyes glowed blue as she patted the first on the back and made a soft chirring noise.

"Um… Apology accepted?" Lily said.

"You are most kind." The first bowed even lower, then straightened.

Lily stifled what would certainly come out as a hysterical laugh. She took a deep breath, then let it out slowly.

I can handle this.

"Where are your manners?" Nana's voice carried to them from somewhere near the couch. "Invite them in."

Lily stepped back from the door and gestured inside. The ant people nodded to her as they passed. Their heads rotated at bizarre angles as they looked all around the room.

"More friends of yours?" Lily said.

Nana laughed. "I sure as hell hope so."

Did Nana not know them? Lily knew she should be scared, but the giant ant aliens had been so terrified of her. She felt more sorry for them than anything else.

"Freddie will not leave my lap," Cyan said, once more trying to lift the cat. He rolled onto his back and stretched. Cyan settled back against the cushions.

"I'm surprised he's staying so calm with all the screaming around here." Nana glared at Lily.

"I'd like to see *you* hold it together if you opened the door to—" Lily cut herself off. She didn't want to hurt the ant people's feelings. Besides, Nana probably wouldn't have been surprised at all.

How had they gotten mixed up in all this?

"I'm Nana," Nana said. "That's my granddaughter, Lily,

and this is my friend, Cyan." Nana pointed to Lily and Cyan in turn.

The ants bowed again, the lights of their eyes dimming for a moment until they stood.

"We are grateful to meet you," the first ant said. She was a bit taller than the second, but otherwise, they looked identical.

"I am Sister," the second ant said. She gestured toward the first ant—the one who had been utterly horrified by Lily's appearance. "And this is Sister."

"You're both named 'Sister'?" Lily asked.

"No, she is Sister and that is Sister." Cyan pointed to the ants, but the names still sounded the same to Lily.

"It can be difficult for translators to pick up the difference," the second ant said.

"Maybe we should call one of you 'Sis' for short," Nana said.

The ants both cocked their heads at her, their eyes doing the strobe thing again, only much slower and with dimmer lights.

"I am the shorter one," the second ant said. "If that is a factor in selecting the abbreviated name."

"That's not what she... Nevermind." Lily shook her head, then pointed to the second ant and then the first. "We'll call you Sis and you Sister, if that's okay with you both."

"I like it," the first—Sister—said.

"Now that we have the names out of the way, what can we do for you?" Nana said. "It's not every day a pair of Antareans show up on my doorstep."

"*Ant*areans?" Lily said. "Really?"

"They're from Antares-3." Nana waved a hand at Lily. "The universe is big enough for plenty of coincidences."

Lily shook her head, but kept her silence. The situation was starting to feel more like a dream again.

"We seek the assistance of the Earthling called Lillian," Sis said.

"That's me." Nana hooked a thumb toward her chest. "Lillian's my given name, but everyone calls me Nana."

Sis and Sister bowed lower than before, their arms held in front of them in the Praying Mantis pose. They stayed that way as Sis said, "Our most humble apologies for the intrusion. We would not have come unannounced if we did not face such dire circumstances. Barbara said you might be able to help us."

Nana let out a little snort. "And *she* couldn't?"

"She has aligned herself with Earth's first contact committee," Sis said. "Because of this, she has pulled back from her distribution operations. If she is discovered providing unauthorized items to planetary systems in need, her altruistic activities could present an obstacle to the High Council recognizing the Department of Homeworld Security."

"The what?" Lily asked.

"The Department of Homeworld Security." This time, it was Cyan who spoke. "Rin and I are also allied with them. We are hoping to further peace and prosperity on your planet and beyond."

"That's…nice, I guess," Lily said. "But why would altruistic activities be an obstacle to anything?"

Nana snorted again. "Because they're not legal. I've been helping Barbara with her trade operation for a while now. The High Council calls it 'smuggling'."

"What?" The skin on Lily's back prickled. "How can the High Council make it illegal to help people?"

"Because the Coalition are the bad guys."

Lily turned to see Rin standing in the open doorway, his expression as grim as his pronouncement. She'd never seen him look so serious.

"The Coalition of Planets?" Lily's feeling of dread increased. "But you're one of their soldiers."

"And that's exactly why I know what I'm talking about," he said.

Chapter Ten

The look on Lily's face felt worse than the burrs Rin had picked out of his feet *and* the cat attack. But she needed to know the truth. They all did.

He walked past a pair of Antareans—who the hell knew why they were here—and nodded toward them. "Sisters."

They nodded back, then straightened, their antennae twitching in his direction. No doubt, they were trying to sort through his pheromones to see if he was friend or foe.

"The Earthlings are calling me Sis," the shorter one said. She pointed to the other. "And she is Sister."

"I guess that saves on confusion." Rin plopped down in the closest chair to the door and rested his feet on a footstool. "It would be nice if the Coalition invested more resources in fine-tuning Antarean translators so we could actually hear the differences in your names. Oh, but wait. They're all assholes."

"You are Sadirian," Sis said. "Part of the Coalition."

"I am."

She tilted her head toward her shoulder farther than most humanoids could manage without it popping off. "Are you also an 'asshole'?"

Rin let out a deep laugh. "I try not to be."

"Then maybe we should avoid labels." Lily crossed her arms over her chest, glaring at him again. He was kind of starting to like it when she did that. At least it meant that she cared.

Sis took a tentative step closer. He hated that she seemed afraid of him, but couldn't blame her for it.

"You are injured," she said.

Rin waved his hand dismissively. "I had a run-in with the cats earlier."

Sis shook her head. "This is more recent. Your chemical trail is laced with pain."

"Did you hurt yourself again?" Lily stalked over to him.

"I wouldn't call being attacked by a bunch of feral cats and then walking through some sort of torture field 'hurting *myself*'," he said.

"Torture field..." Lily looked at his feet, then let out an exasperated sigh. "You ran around outside barefoot."

"A mistake I swear not to make again," he said.

She dropped to her knees next to the footstool and started inspecting his feet, muttering "Tourists" under her breath. Her touch was gentle as she ran her thumbs over the surface of his skin, pressing different spots as if checking to make sure he hadn't left any parts of the burrs behind. He'd been careful not to when he removed them, but he was enjoying her touch too much to say anything.

"We can also assist," Sis said. She moved closer, but then balked, her antennae straightening briefly as she stepped back. "Or...not."

"Don't worry about him," Nana said. "Rin's one of the good guys."

"That is not why... Um..." Sis stammered, her translator failing to make sense of her string of clicks. "There is a rather strong pheromone field around them."

He didn't doubt it. The level of attraction he felt for Lily was...

"Wait," Rin said. "'Them'? As in both of us?"

Sis's eyes glowed a rosy pink and she angled her head away.

Lily looked up from her inspection of his feet. "What does that mean?"

Rin grinned at her. He sidestepped Lily's question with one of his own. "So, Nana, do you run a boarding house for aliens or something?"

Nana laughed. "No, but—"

"Don't give her any ideas." Lily stood, hovering close to Rin's side. She even rested her hand on the back of his chair. "The Antareans think Nana can help them with something. What is it that you need?"

There was an earnestness in her tone that made Rin's heart skip. Most people would be freaking out about now, but Lily seemed to be taking all of this in stride. More than that, she sounded like she wanted to help.

He reached up and gripped her hand, giving it a squeeze before bringing it down to rest on his shoulder and holding it there. He heard a little intake of breath from her, but she didn't pull away.

"Thank you for hearing us," Sister said. Her eyes pulsed a dull yellow—an Antarean biosignal for anguish and fear that made Rin's heart ache.

Sis stood a little straighter, her translator pausing intermittently as it processed her communications. "An outbreak of fungus is spreading rapidly among our colonies. It weakens the joints of our carapaces to the point that our limbs are easily broken off. Though we have many limbs, those afflicted often lose enough that they must be reassigned to less strenuous tasks, lest they lose all they have."

"Well, crap," Nana said. "You don't have to tell me more to convince me to help. I sure as hell wouldn't want to have to sit around all day hoping my arms wouldn't fall off."

Lily's voice was calm and focused when she spoke up. "How is my Nana supposed to help you? I mean, she's one Earthling and it sounds like you're talking about helping a huge amount of people."

"There is a substance on Earth that is known to strengthen the chitin that makes up our shells," Sis said. "From the few transmissions we have been able to analyze from Earth, we believe it is undesirable for you, but it is especially effective on the softer sections that make up our joints. It is a binder protein that is common in your food but rare on our planet."

"A binder protein?" Lily asked.

"Yes." Sis nodded. "I believe it is called gluten."

Lily let out a brief laugh. "I'm sorry. Did you say 'gluten'?"

"Barbara has confirmed that its molecular structure is compatible with our physiology," Sister said. "It has a long-term effect. Your advertisements often speak positively of foods being 'gluten-free'. We do not have much to offer in trade, but were hopeful that you might be willing to part with some of your discarded gluten."

"I don't think that's how it works." Nana's voice was gentler than Lily was used to hearing it. "Those foods are made from substances that just don't have that particular protein in them."

"Oh," Sister said. "We thought…" Her antennae slumped against her head, the lights in her eyes dimming.

Sis rested several of her hands on Sister's back. "We appreciate you hearing us—"

"Hold on." Lily's grip on Rin's shoulder tightened. He squeezed her hand back, hoping to encourage her with… whatever she was doing.

"That doesn't mean we can't help you." Lily looked over at Nana, who nodded at her.

"Our family runs an import/export company," Lily said.

"This is what I do. I've seen gluten for sale in the baked goods aisle. With our resources and contacts, it should be a simple matter to set up a supply stream, depending on how much you need."

The Antareans exchanged a glance, then turned back to Lily. "As I said, we have limited resources with which to trade—"

"I don't care," Lily said. "Just tell me how much is required to treat everyone right now, and then we can work together to figure out a plan going forward."

Rin felt his heart pounding in his chest. She was speaking with utter conviction. If it was possible, he fully believed she would find a way to help them. He wondered if she would even bother negotiating for anything in return.

In all the years he'd served the Coalition, all the stations and planets he'd visited and sentients he'd met, he'd never heard such a generous offer. He'd never felt as keenly someone else's desire to help others, no matter what.

Except from his own heart.

Sis pulled in a breath with a whistling sound. She held it for a moment, then said, "Two thousand pounds."

Lily stilled. Rin didn't know anything about gluten. Was that a lot?

"Two thousand pounds," she repeated. "Are you certain you understand our measurements correctly?"

"We will be able to mix the gluten with materials that we have on our planet, but trace amounts of the protein are vital in creating a treatment. In order to assist everyone in the colonies who have been afflicted, it will take one ton, based on this country's system of communicating weight," Sis said. "We know it is a great deal to ask for."

"It isn't." Lily was beaming when Rin looked up at her. "I can transport that much in my truck."

Nana pulled out her phone and started tapping on the screen. She let out a laugh. "We can cover the purchase with petty cash. Heck, I have enough to pay for it hidden in the filing cabinet in your mom's office."

Lily did a double-take. "You have money hidden in mom's office?"

"You think you're the only one who plans for unexpected eventualities?" Nana laughed. "Cash is the least of what you should be worrying about stumbling across. The point is, this stuff is cheap, compared to what we're usually dealing with."

Sis shook her head. "I don't understand."

Lily squeezed Rin's shoulder tighter. "You'll have what you need by the end of the day."

Chapter Eleven

Lily pulled into the parking lot behind her loft that was reserved for tenants. Her palms were sweating. She didn't think it was just from the heat, especially when she cast a quick glance at the dark haired man sitting next to her.

"You could have stayed back at the bungalow," she said.

Rin smiled at her. "What kind of gentleman would I be if I made you take care of this all yourself?"

"An alien one?"

He laughed, and the smile she'd been fighting finally won.

"'An alien gentleman'," he said. "I like it."

She did, too, not that she was about to admit it.

"We have some time before Julian arrives with the gluten," she said. "Apparently, it wasn't quite as easy as I thought to find a source for a ton of the stuff. He's gathering up what we need and will meet us here in a couple of hours."

"Are we just going to sit here and wait?"

"Of course not." She turned off the truck, then opened the door and hopped to the ground. Rin joined her.

Options ran through her head. Where should she take him? What should they do?

There were plenty of restaurants within walking distance. Stores and cozy spots that she could show him.

"Let's go inside." The words slipped out of her mouth before she could stop them.

That had not been one of the options she was considering. That was the start of the fantasy that she'd been fighting ever since they climbed into the truck and drove off by themselves.

They would walk into her loft. He would close the door, staring meaningfully into her eyes, and then...

"Lily?"

"Huh?"

"You weren't responding."

She shook her head. She had to stop zoning out. "Sorry. There's just a lot on my mind at the moment."

"I don't doubt it." He gestured for her to lead the way.

As they entered the building, he leaned over her shoulder and said, "By the way, I think you're handling all of this amazingly well."

I can think of other things I'd like to handle.

She kicked herself inwardly. Where were these thoughts coming from?

Sure, he was gorgeous and kind and funny. And he was walking really close to her. When he'd leaned down to talk to her, she could feel his breath on the bare skin of her neck. But she had just met him. And he was an *alien*.

He'd probably be flying off into space after they were done delivering these supplies. Which meant there was no chance of attachment.

Sparks kindled in her belly.

No attachments. No complications.

Maybe this was her chance to finally do something spontaneous and crazy, to give in to what she wanted instead of constantly thinking out all the possibilities and coming up with ridiculous amounts of contingency plans. A momentary connection that they could both enjoy and then walk away from.

The risks involved seemed minimal.

She couldn't believe she was even considering this. She had responsibilities. Obligations. She was trying to help an entire species, for crying out loud.

She led Rin up the stairs quickly, then stopped in front of the door at the top. As she unlocked it, she said, "This used to be Nana's loft, but she gave it to me when she moved out of town. There's only the roof above, and the people who live below me are on vacation."

Why was she telling him that?

"I guess we don't have to worry about being interrupted, then." He laughed, but her mind immediately jumped to distracting scenarios.

The door swung open, and her gaze fell on the large bed that dominated the alcove to their right. "Yeah."

He walked into her home, pausing in the center of the space and looking all around. His shirt pulled against the muscles of his back, emphasizing the strong lines of his shoulders and the muscles on his arms. She imagined coming up behind him and wrapping her arms around his narrow waist, reaching to the front of his cargo shorts...

"Lily?" he turned around to face her, which meant, for a moment, she was staring right at his crotch.

She quickly looked up at his face. It was just as stimulating, though. Dark eyes, strong jaw, and a chest she wanted to explore so much that her fingers curled at her sides.

"You were kind of blanking again," he said.

"Yeah. I need to stop doing that."

He laughed. "No worries. I do the same thing. Are you going to come in? You do live here, after all."

"Right." She pushed herself across the threshold, angling away from him as she shut the door.

Her place was actually pretty small, and she didn't entertain...ever. The area that was meant to be the living space was taken up with her home office. There was nowhere to sit.

Except the bed.

She shook herself. There were barstools lining the counter just behind him. That would work.

Out of habit, she kicked off her shoes, then pulled off her socks. Rin watched with one eyebrow arched.

"I usually go barefoot at home," she said.

"Okay." Rin bent down and unlaced his boots. He slid them off, then took off his socks as well.

Great. Now they were getting undressed together. Again.

She felt her cheeks heat at the thought.

She gestured toward the barstools as she approached them. "Have a seat, if you'd like. My place isn't really designed for company."

"I'm good standing after the ride in."

Damn, she had already crossed most of the room and was standing right next to him. It would be awkward if she sat while they talked, right?

"You don't have people over often?" he asked.

"I don't have people over ever."

"That sounds kind of lonely."

"I socialize plenty at work."

"That's not the same." He tucked a strand of hair that had come loose from her ponytail behind her shoulder. His thumb grazed her skin as he pulled his hand back.

Fireworks ignited low in her belly. Tingling pleasure shot along her nerves and gathered between her legs. They were standing so close that she could feel the heat radiating from him.

"Camaraderie is great, but it's not the same as companionship," he said.

"I don't really have time for relationships."

"Relationships?"

She needed to steer the conversation back to safer ground. What had she been thinking, indulging in those fantasies before?

"Some connections form quickly," he said. "They don't require that much time to develop."

"They probably end just as fast."

"Not necessarily."

"Relationships take time to cultivate and nurture." Her voice grew stronger. She wished her resolve would as well.

"That's true. But it's worth it to be surrounded by people who appreciate and support you."

"I have people who appreciate me."

"Let me guess. At work?"

She glared at him in response.

Apparently, he wasn't cowed. "Work relationships probably feel safer. You can't get too intimate, or there may be complications. Your family owns the company, so you're also in a position of power, and I'm betting you're the kind of person who would never cross that boundary."

"I thought you were a field medic, not a psychologist."

"I'm a—" He cut himself off, then shook his head with a sigh. "I've studied many human cultures, including yours. And I'm as close to being a human as you're likely to find among my kind."

"Among a bunch of Sadirians who've had their emotions turned off?"

"Only a few of them have, and that was on my previous

ship, the *Reckoning*." He flinched when he said the word.

Lily was sure the person behind his own trust issues—Clara—was stationed on that ship.

"Have you made friends on your new ship? Formed any…relationships?"

He smiled. "A few. Superficial at best."

"Sounds lonely."

He was quiet for a moment, then said, "There's a reason I understand you. At least, I think I do."

She couldn't deny it. Instead, she said, "You just met me."

"Some connections form quickly."

"Not this quickly." She didn't want complications. She didn't want anything she had to think through. Did she?

"You can't just bury yourself in your work and expect to be happy without ever taking a break to really bond with anyone."

She looked away, but he reached for her again. This time, he caught her chin in his hand and gently urged her to look at him.

Ignoring the warmth that rippled through her at his touch, the pleasure humming along her nerves, she said, "My work is important."

"So is this."

Chapter Twelve

Rin couldn't believe what he was doing, but the pull toward Lily beckoned like the gravity of a neutron star. He leaned forward, brushing her lips lightly with his.

Before he could do more, she closed the distance between them, wrapping her arms around his neck and pressing her body against his. Those soft, warm lips caught his in a kiss that sent streams of energy coursing through his body.

Her tongue traced his mouth. He opened himself to her with a moan that echoed through his chest. She stroked him hungrily, igniting a need in him to be closer, to hold her tighter, to explore as much of her as he could.

He grabbed her ass, lifting her from the ground. As she wrapped her legs around his waist, he explored her mouth with his kiss, taking the lead in their passionate sparring.

The bed was close. He carried her to it and lowered her to the sand colored sheets.

His dick pressed against her core. They were wearing too many clothes.

He knelt between her legs, parting from her for just long

enough to tear his shirt over his head and toss it on the floor. She took the opportunity to do the same.

Her breasts were bared to him, small and perfect. He leaned back down, taking one tight brown peak between his lips.

"Rin." She gasped his name, her fingers burrowing through his hair.

How could hearing her say his name hit his system like a shock cannon?

His nerves were electrified, his skin covered in goosebumps. He undid the fasteners for her shorts, loosening them enough that he could push them down, then cast them away.

Seeing her naked before him, feeling her skin, tasting her... He couldn't seem to find words.

He leaned forward and kissed her stomach, her hip, working his way to the soft patch of curls that invited his attention. Pushing her legs apart, he brought his lips to her clit, drawing on all of the knowledge he'd gained studying Earthlings before his assignment.

She gasped. "I'm not...usually...like this," she managed, between deep, panting breaths.

He paused just long enough to say, "Neither am I."

He ran one of his fingers down her slit, wetting it before plunging it deep inside her. Her back arched, and she grabbed fistfuls of the sheets.

Her pussy was tight. So tight. When he buried his dick

in her, it would be heaven. He just had to make sure it was heaven for her, too.

Another finger joined the first, and he pressed his lips to her clit again. She writhed on the bed, hips gyrating against him as he matched her movements with his hand.

"Oh God," she said.

He increased the pressure with his lips, spread his fingers to stretch her, quickened the pace of his strokes. His dick was throbbing, chafing against the constraint of his cargo shorts.

"Rin!"

He felt her pulse around him as she screamed his name, her hips thrashing. A fierce emotion flooded through him as he drew out her climax, his fingers continuing to move in her, his lips tight on her clit.

She sank back into the mattress and he finally slowed his pace.

He had never done anything like that before. Never experienced such closeness. He was a little bit in awe that he could bring another person such pleasure with nothing but himself.

And not just anyone.

He had shared a moment unlike any other in his life with the kindest, most generous, and confident human he'd encountered on Earth. He had shared that connection with Lily.

He stood and took a step back from the bed. His hands

were shaking.

She looked at him through heavy-lidded eyes. "Are you okay?"

"I don't know." He shook his head. Is this what it had felt like for the others? Was this the reason so many of his colleagues had pair-bonded so quickly?

"I want..." His voice trailed off. Too many things ran through his mind. Scenarios that he would most likely never get to experience.

And the siren call of what was right in front of him.

He wanted to throw himself on her, to bury himself in her. He'd never wanted anything more.

Lily scooted to the end of the bed and reached out to hook her fingers in his waistband and pull him closer. "I 'want', too."

She undid his shorts, holding his gaze the entire time. Her cheeks were flushed, as was the skin of her neck and chest. There were marks where he'd kissed her. Had he really left them?

Cool air hit his dick as she pulled down his cargo shorts and boxer briefs at the same time. He stepped out of them just before she wrapped her hand around his shaft.

His lungs stopped working. He couldn't make his chest move to pull in air. All he could do was stand there as his muscles tightened, his entire focus of existence centering on her hand touching him.

She tightened her grip, stroking the length of him, then

ran her thumb over the tip of his crown, collecting the bead of moisture that had gathered there.

"I can't resist you," she murmured.

"Mutual," was all he could manage.

She grinned up at him, perhaps the first complete smile he'd seen from her. His heart pounded. At least he could manage quick shallow breaths. He was going to hyperventilate at this rate.

"Cyan said you've all been checked to be sure you're not carrying harmful pathogens," Lily said.

Rin nodded. "Yes."

"I'm on birth control," she said. "And I've also been recently cleared of having Earth pathogens."

"Does that mean you want to—"

"I really, really want to."

The breath pent up in his chest rushed out. He was about to push her back on the bed and drive himself into her, but she had other ideas. She slid to her knees in front of him. Before he could speculate about what she was doing, she wrapped her lips around his crown.

"Fuck." A torrent of sensation crashed along his nerves, flooding his body with pleasure.

She looked up at him with a smirk. "Soon."

Her lips wrapped around him again, tighter. She flicked her tongue along the length of his shaft as she took him deeper into her mouth.

A throbbing began in his dick. Heat and tingling energy

building deep in his abdomen.

"Lily," he warned.

She pulled away from him and stood, turning him so that his back was toward the bed, then she pushed on his shoulders. He let himself fall.

Lily crawled along with him as he shifted up closer to the pillows, her hands and knees on either side of his body. As soon as he'd settled, she returned her attention to his dick, gripping it in her hand and swirling its tip with her tongue.

He tried to think about scan readouts, star maps, anything but the steady pulse of pleasure beating through his nerves in time with his pounding heart. Finally, she released him, kissing a path up his abdomen. His breath eased a bit at the gentler sensations that brought on, until she brought her hips down against his, pressing his dick into her slit.

"You're sure you want—" His words turned to a grunt as she slid her labia along his length.

Wet. Warmth. And then he was poised at her core.

"Yes." Her voice became tentative, as she asked, "Are you?"

"I've never wanted anything more. Or anyone."

Her eyes widened as if she was surprised.

"I mean it." He gripped her hips, and slowly guided her down over his shaft.

She leaned back on her knees, straddling him, letting

him sink in deep. If they'd gone faster, he would have climaxed immediately. Instead, he was able to savor the sensation, feel her parting for him, her pussy so tight around him.

She rested her hands on his stomach as her eyes rolled shut briefly. Then she smiled at him and said, "Mutual."

Chapter Thirteen

Lily was having sex with an alien. An alien she had just met.

That should bother her, but it didn't. It was hard for anything to bother her as she paused for a moment to let her body acclimate to him.

Rin, inside her. Filling her.

After the last orgasm, her nerves were poised for more. Every little movement sent tendrils of pleasure curling out through her limbs.

He had his hands on her hips still—those gorgeous hands. He massaged her hips, the movement both relaxing and stimulating, as it caused subtle shifts in where they were joined.

He wasn't rushing her. He wasn't ignoring her as he chased his own pleasure.

Being with Rin... Everything about it felt right.

Except he was an alien. She doubted he'd be staying on Earth forever. She'd thought that was a good thing when she decided to "be spontaneous". Now, she wasn't sure.

"Are you okay?" he asked.

"What? Oh, yeah." She let out a small laugh. "I overthink things even at the worst times."

Like in the middle of what had started off as incredibly hot sex.

"Don't think," he said. He shifted his hips up, pressing into her more deeply. "Feel."

She nodded, shoving away all the thoughts of complications and plans and worry about the future. Working together, they were going to help an entire species. And in the meantime, they could enjoy this moment, however long it lasted.

She lifted herself up onto her knees, sliding along his shaft. As she let herself sink back down, he groaned, his eyes squeezing shut. He seemed to be savoring everything as much as she was.

"Thank you," he said.

She laughed again. She couldn't actually remember ever laughing before during sex. The movement sent delicious tendrils of pleasure unfurling through her belly.

"For what?" she asked.

"For going slow. I want this to last."

"We have a couple of hours," she said, lifting herself back up, feeling every inch of him. "We can always do it again."

His eyes snapped open. "Again?"

Lily half-shrugged as she lowered herself, taking him in deep. She licked her lips, imagining scenarios that were so much better than the plans and budgets that normally filled her mind.

"And maybe again-again," she said.

They could shower together. She could take him in her mouth—share that experience. They could do all sorts of things.

Rin seemed to consider her words. "Then maybe we don't need to hold back."

Her heart was already pounding. It seemed to kick into even higher gear at his words.

"I'd rather you didn't," she said. Her core clenched around him. He was stretching her so much.

"Lily…"

He sat up, running his hands along her back, then claimed her mouth again. He rolled them over, his weight pressing her into the bed. Grabbing her thigh, he pulled her leg up until it wrapped around his ass, pushing his dick even deeper.

She gasped as he thrust his hips, harder and faster. He moved his mouth to her neck. His teeth grazed her skin with a tantalizing pressure that sent goosebumps streaking over her body.

His chest moved against hers, his soft hair teasing her nipples. It was as if he didn't want any space between them. Pressure built deep in her belly, her core tightened around him, making each stroke resonate through her.

She brought her arms up along his sides, raked her nails

down his spine, then squeezed his ass. He groaned, increasing his pace, rocking against her so hard the bed shook.

Fireworks started to erupt deep within her, a chain reaction that set her senses on fire. She cried out his name, just as she felt his dick start to pulse.

He kept on pounding into her, spilling himself, drawing out her orgasm just as he'd done before. Finally, he slowed, then stopped, his dick buried deep. Her pussy was still throbbing, echoing the pulse of his shaft. She had never felt so deliciously satisfied.

His breath fanned her neck as he rested for a moment. He pressed his hips against hers more firmly, kissing his way back to her mouth.

Lily hadn't thought her senses could take more, but when he slid his tongue into her mouth—languidly thrusting, tasting, teasing—she felt more electric tingles spread from where they were joined. Finally, he lifted himself on his elbows and stared down at her.

"So…" he said. "Again?"

She burst out laughing.

Hours later, after the most amazing shower ever, Lily drove them back toward Nana's house, her truck filled with bags of gluten. Julian had worked with Nana long enough to know when to not ask questions. He just smiled and shook his head after helping them load everything.

Rin glanced at his watch, then said, "The Antareans' ship is a little ways past Nana's house. That's where they're waiting for us."

"Okay."

Their ship. As in *spaceship.*

Lily's stomach did flips at the thought. She was about to see a real-life alien spaceship. Heck, she was making a delivery to it.

If she had her way, this would be the first of many similar occasions.

She wasn't sure how she could get in touch with aliens that she could help, though. From what Rin had told her about the Coalition, there had to be more people out there in dire need.

Maybe I could ask him to help me. Maybe somehow he could stay.

The thought was tempting. Rin didn't try to hide how unhappy he was with the Coalition. And he seemed to be happy with her. He made *her* happy.

But how could they be together when he was a soldier in an alien space fleet?

"This is the turn," Rin said.

He pointed to a small road that veered off from the packed sand street they'd been driving down. She managed to navigate the turn, praying that her wheels wouldn't get stuck in the softer sand of the side road. Branches scraped along her truck as they bounced over the uneven terrain. They weren't very far from Nana's house.

"Well, this is fun." Rin was grinning when she glanced at him.

"You and I have very different ideas of fun."

He leaned over and kissed the side of her neck. "I don't know about that."

She could feel her cheeks heating even in the humid summer air. Thoughts of their time in her apartment pushed into her mind, distracting her.

"Um, Lily?" Rin said. "That's the ship."

She slammed on the brakes, throwing sand up into the wheel wells. Not the best idea if she didn't want to get stuck.

"Wait…" Looking around, all she saw was a termite mound. A giant termite mound, like she'd seen in documentaries about Africa. Sis and Sister would barely fit inside it, let alone all the gluten in the bed of her truck. "That's the ship?"

"Part of it." Rin opened his door and jumped out. "Most of it is underground."

A crack appeared in the center of the structure. It widened, revealing an opening big enough for Lily to walk through.

Two Antareans stepped out of it, one after another. And

then another Antarean. And then another. And another—until the clearing was filled with at least two dozen of the ant people. There must be a heck of a lot of ship buried under the ground.

Lily knew she should be afraid, but she wasn't. Especially when Nana and Cyan stepped out of the ship. The Antareans parted to let them through, then stepped close again so that they were surrounding Lily and her small group, forming two perfect circles.

A pair of Antareans approached, one slightly shorter than the other. Sis and Sister? If Lily was going to work with aliens, she was going to have to learn how to tell them all apart.

The shorter one bowed low. "Was your expedition successful?"

"Yes." Lily pointed to her truck. "The gluten's there in the truck. It's all yours."

The Antareans started making a loud clicking/hissing sound, their antennae moving in quick, intricate patterns on their heads. Their eyes strobed blue and white as they... talked to each other?

"They seem pretty excited," Lily murmured, shifting closer to Rin.

"Wouldn't you be?" He smiled down at her, finding her hand and clasping it in his.

The Antarean Lily was pretty sure was Sis made a high-pitched whistling noise and all the others calmed, staring at her intently. She made a series of clicks and pops, then gestured to Lily.

They turned to her and bowed. All of them. Their antennae nearly touching the ground.

"We have nothing with which to trade," Sis said, "So we offer ourselves in service."

"What?" Lily shook her head, dropping Rin's hand as she stepped forward. "No. No way."

She reached toward Sis and rested her hands on her... carapace, urging her to stand.

"There are no strings attached to this," Lily said.

Sis tilted her head to the side, her eyes flickering pale green. "Strings?"

Dang, Lily needed to stop using idioms.

"I don't want anything in return," Lily said. "This is a gift."

The green of Sis's eyes turned a bit olive and the flickering slowed. She bowed her head, and said, "There are always strings. Always 'wants'."

Lily's cheeks heated as she thought back to her conversation with Rin about what they wanted. Sis was right. Everyone had an agenda.

Lily wanted more from Rin. More time, more... connection. She wanted a chance to see if there was something between them beyond this incredible chemistry. And she wanted something from the Antareans as well.

"You're right," Lily said. "I do want something. I'm

only just realizing it now."

Sis stood a bit straighter, her eyes locked in that murky green color, as if she was bracing herself for whatever Lily was about to say.

"I want us to be friends," Lily said. "And...allies. I need someone to help me reach others who are in need, like your people. That doesn't mean you have to be the ones to do it. You can just...point me in the right direction or something. Hook me up with somebody like this Barbara person you mentioned, but who isn't concerned with the stupid High Council."

Rin snickered, then tried to mask it with a fake cough. Lily grinned at him and shook her head.

"This is what you ask in trade?" Sis said.

"No. I don't ask anything in trade. I'm giving you this gluten. I don't have limitless resources, but giving you this does me no harm, and keeping it to myself would have terrible repercussions for your people. I couldn't live with myself if I didn't help." Lily let out an exasperated breath. "You owe me nothing."

Sis cocked her head to the side again, her eyes flickering. The light morphed from green to pale yellow.

"I only told you what I want because you asked," Lily said. "And if we're going to be friends, we need to talk to each other and learn about each other. So...now you know."

Lily shrugged. She stared at Sis, holding her breath.

Sis reached out with one of her arms and rested it on Lily's shoulder. "To be friends with such a generous being would bring me great joy. And I express my deepest gratitude for this gift. We accept your offer and your alliance, and stand ready to assist you in your goal."

They were going to assist… Lily couldn't believe it. She'd just established a potential partner in helping people throughout the freaking galaxy.

When she'd set her sights on using the import/export company for altruistic pursuits, she had no idea they would be so expansive.

Her heart was pounding. She felt a little dizzy, even. She wanted to shout and laugh and cry all at once.

Instead, she cleared her throat, trying to control the emotions that threatened to overwhelm her. This was the most important moment in her life.

Well, one of them.

She glanced over her shoulder at Rin. He was beaming at her.

"Okay then," Lily said. "We'll be in touch…somehow, I guess."

Rin stepped forward. "I'd be happy to help."

"The Coalition won't be okay with that," Lily said.

"What the Coalition doesn't know…" He winked at her, and she laughed, despite her worry for him. "Come on, Sis. We'll set up a secure channel while the other Sisters load the ship. Cyan, do you mind helping us out?"

"I am very pleased to assist all my friends." She looked up at him, a wide smile stretching across her face.

The three of them walked a few steps away from Lily, messing with Rin's watch and talking in hushed tones. The Antareans formed a line between the ship and the truck, passing the heavy bags of gluten over their heads.

"Now that's efficiency for you." Nana walked over to Lily and wrapped an arm around her shoulder. "We could use help like this in the warehouses."

"Nana—"

"For good pay." Nana clucked at her. "Alliances and trades are strongest when we help each other. It's best for both parties. But this…" Her eyes followed the trail of bags disappearing into the ship. "This is something else. A really good something else. I'm proud of you."

Lily's eyes misted over. "Thanks."

"And happy for you, too." Nana leaned in close and whispered, "He's a real hottie."

"Nana!" Lily said, then laughed.

Lily was happy for herself. Happier than she'd been in a very long time.

If Rin was going to help her communicate with the Antareans, that meant they would be keeping in touch as well. And she really enjoyed the thought of keeping in touch with him.

Rin, Cyan, and Sis headed back to Nana and Lily. As soon as he was close enough, Rin claimed Lily's hand again, interlacing their fingers.

"We have a secured channel set up between Cyan and the Antareans," Rin said. "We'll get a communications device set up at Nana's place, and use it to coordinate, if that's okay."

"Fine with me," Nana said.

"And, of course, Cyan and I will need to keep visiting to set things up and check on the equipment." Rin smiled down at Lily.

"I have a feeling Cyan and I will be going for lots of walks during those visits," Nana said.

Cyan cocked her head to the side. "Why is that?"

"Pheromones," Nana said.

Sis let out a chittering that sounded suspiciously like a laugh. Her eyes pulsed pink.

"It would be safest for everyone to clear the area before we launch," Sis said. She turned to Lily and bowed her head slightly, but only for a moment. "We will not forget what you have done for us. And we thank you."

"I'm glad I could help," Lily said.

Nana gestured in the direction of her house. "Let's go ahead and walk back to my place. It isn't far. These two can take the truck."

"Come on," Rin said. "The sooner they head out, the sooner they can begin treating their people."

"Right." Lily waved one last time at Sis before climbing into the truck and heading back to the road that would take them to Nana's.

Chapter Fourteen

"That was really incredible," Lily said.

"You have no idea." Rin was still trying to process everything.

She had saved an entire species from a plague. And he had helped her do it. They were setting up a system to help even more sentients in the galaxy.

For the first time in as long as he could remember, Rin felt...meaningful. He had purpose, beyond what was assigned to him. And a lot of that purpose was building around the beautiful woman beside him.

"Lily, I want..." He paused, not sure how to put his thoughts into words without scaring her off.

"Sounds good to me." Lily laughed, then pulled her truck to the side of the road and parked it, shutting off the engine.

She turned to him with a smile that promised things. Wonderful things.

He shifted in his seat, focusing on what he needed to say before anything else could happen between them.

"We need to talk," he said.

"Oh." Lily sat back, a worried look on her face. "You know, on Earth, when someone says, 'We need to talk', it's almost always a bad thing."

"It isn't. I hope not, anyway. I just need you to know what you're getting into."

Shit, *was* this a bad thing?

He sighed. "I know you have your business and your mission. I want to help you as much as I can, but I have to be careful. If the Coalition catches you helping others, I'm not sure what they'll do."

"Won't they just give me a mind-wipe?"

"That's what the law would tell them to do."

She nodded slowly. "But you're not sure they would follow the law."

"There's more risk here than you realize," he said.

"It's worth it, but…"

He waited a few moments before prompting her to continue. "'But'?"

"What will happen to *you* if they catch us? You're a Coalition soldier, and you're defying them to help me."

"I'm defying them to help sentients who desperately need it. And to do what I know in my heart is right." He lifted her hand and placed it on his chest. Warmth spread through him at her touch, at the way she smiled softly up at him and splayed her fingers over his heart.

"I'm being really selfish," she said.

"What?"

He couldn't understand how she could think such a thing. She'd been nothing but generous in everything he'd seen her do. Helping Cyan and the Antareans. And when they'd made love at her apartment... Selfish was not a word he would associate with her.

"I want...more," she said.

He racked his brain trying to think of what she could mean. More resources? More access to tech?

She reached up to put her hand on the back of his neck and pulled him in for a kiss. Slow and lingering, then deeper as she shifted closer. She crawled across the bench seat, straddling him.

Time seemed to dilate until all he knew was her and this. Their kiss, their bodies pressed together, mouths dancing, tongues exploring.

Eventually, she pulled back, tracing his cheek with her fingertips.

"I want you," she said.

He didn't hesitate in his response. "You have me."

"No, I mean, I want more than this. I want to get to know you. I want to spend time with you. But every moment we're together, it adds to your risk of being discovered."

"It's worth it." He let out a sigh, knowing he had to tell her more if they were really going to do any of this together. Explore their connection. Help other sentients. "Things might get harder than you think."

She leaned forward and nipped at his ear, sending jolts of pleasure through him. "Oh, I'm counting on that," she said.

Rin let out a little laugh, despite his fear for their situation. "That's not what I'm talking about. I want all those things with you, too. But the Coalition is sending the *Reckoning* to assess the situation here on Earth. It's a warship scheduled to arrive within weeks."

"Oh. That is bad." She pulled back and stared at him, all hint of humor gone. "Wait, what 'situation' are they assessing?"

"Other species are trespassing here. We don't know how many. And Earthlings aren't supposed to know we exist, let alone be pair-bonding with us."

"Pair-bonding?"

"Like marriage, only with less joy and more paperwork."

"Fun." She was quiet for a moment, her eyes narrowing as she thought things through. "When the ship arrives, will it take you all away?"

"That's the best-case scenario." He had to be honest with her—and himself. "Worst case, they'll think Earth is ready to be brought into the Coalition, and it'll be stripped of resources in exchange for access to our technology."

"How can anyone think that's a fair trade?"

"The tech is alluring. Extremely long lifespans. No sickness." He smirked. "No allergies."

"Except, Cyan does have allergies. And even with your tech, you were nearly taken down by…"

Lily twisted around and opened a compartment in the front of the vehicle. She pulled out a cylinder of those damned "cat treats".

"Are you insane?" Rin grabbed her hands, holding them still to keep the container from making any noise. "Those cats are still out there, and we're close enough to Nana's for them to hear."

"Relax, I just—"

His watch emitted a loud, keening beep. A proximity alert. Sadirian tech was nearby, and it wasn't being used by anyone in the Department of Homeworld Security.

Oh shit. It's too soon.

Lily covered her ears, wincing. "What is that?"

Rin lifted her from his lap and opened the door to the truck. He flung himself to the ground. Panic clouded his thoughts. He had to keep Lily safe—and Nana. Distance was his only option.

"Coalition soldiers," Rin yelled. "You have to go. Get to Nana and take her as far away from here as you can."

"Rin—"

"Warn Cyan."

He turned to run and made it three strides away before he felt his muscles seize up, his body freezing in place. A stasis field.

"Rin!" If anything, Lily's voice sounded closer. She was

supposed to be running away. She was supposed to be saving herself.

Of course, Lily didn't run. She wouldn't leave him—or anyone—helpless. But she had no idea what she was dealing with.

The *Reckoning*. It was here.

He wondered how many had been sent after him. A full landing party or just a few soldiers? He didn't have to wait long to find out.

A single Sadirian stepped out of the trees surrounding them. Her silver uniform clung to her body—an efficient choice rather than an aesthetic one. She held her left arm out toward him, her bracer generating the stasis field that held him. With her right hand, she hit the button on her collar that controlled her helmet.

Inch-wide segments appeared in the shiny chrome. They folded back on themselves, sliding into the compartment around her neck and revealing her face.

Shining chestnut hair. Pale skin. Deep brown eyes. Features he knew by heart.

Clara...

Why the hell had she come? And by herself?

"I always knew you were overly emotional, but I had no idea you were stupid, too," she said.

"Hey!" Lily yelled.

Rin's heart sank. Lily was heading for a mind-wipe. There was no way around it. She would forget him and the

Antareans and all about the chance she had to make a difference in the galaxy. Clara would take that from her. From both of them.

"Come here, Earthling," Clara commanded. "Or I'll vaporize your transport with you in it."

He heard Lily climb down from the truck, but couldn't turn to see her, couldn't warn her. He couldn't do anything.

He grit his teeth together, wishing he could speak, could swear, could...throw sand in Clara's face to distract her for long enough to let Lily escape.

But there was no escape. Rin wasn't fool enough to think otherwise.

Clara would take them both back to her ship. Hopefully, she didn't know about Nana and no one was heading toward Nana's house.

Then again, if they ran into Cyan, maybe Rin and Lily would stand a chance. The Coalition had done next to nothing to improve on the technology the Vegans had given them. Meanwhile the Vegans had spent the thousands of years since making advances.

But Cyan was with Nana at the house. As close as they were, it was still too far to call out to her. Cyan was keeping her exosuit as dormant as possible to avoid detection. She wouldn't know that Clara was there.

The only comfort Rin had was knowing what a surprise the *Reckoning's* soldiers would get when they tried to take in the others. The Vegans would stop them, and the

Coalition would know they'd finally met their match.

"Step away from the transport." Clara started to reach for the plasma pistol strapped to her thigh. Lily must have done something to set her off.

Please, please, don't set her off.

"Okay, you caught me," Lily said.

"I have. And your transport has been thoroughly scanned. I know that you are without weapons."

"That's great. Then you know that this thing is harmless."

Rin heard a rattling sound that sent a shiver down his spine. The can of cat treats. What was Lily doing?

"What is that?" Clara demanded.

"It's just a...musical instrument," Lily said. "I was showing it to Rin when you interrupted us. That's considered really rude on this planet, by the way."

"I have no concern for the cultural norms of your primitive planet."

"That is no way to start off with a new trade partner."

Clara bristled. "We are not trade partners."

"So, the Coalition has no interest in Earth's resources?" Lily said. "Or working with someone who already has established contacts and methods for gaining access to goods from all over the world?"

Clara's eyes narrowed.

Lily continued, a confidence ringing through her tone that he'd never heard before. "I don't know if your laws insist on working through planetary governments—which could be a problem for you, since we have a ton of those that you'll have to learn to work with individually. But I would think the High Council would at least want to consider working with a single entity who already has systems in place to get them *anything they want.*"

Clever.

Lily knew the Coalition was interested in Earth's resources. Hell, she might even mean what she was saying —to a point.

"You can explain this all to my commanding officer," Clara said. "We are leaving."

"That sounds great." Lily had walked far enough forward that Rin could see her. She actually smiled. "But you should know something about my personal 'cultural norms'."

Clara waited for Lily to continue. After a few moments of uncomfortable silence, she said, "Which are?"

"I like to welcome people with gifts."

Clara shifted her weight so that it was balanced more easily between both feet. She could react to anything, was ready for whatever Lily threw at her.

She threw the can. Rin heard the rattling of the treats as it flew over his head.

"Here you go," Lily said.

Clara caught the can out of the air easily with her right hand. She eyed it suspiciously.

"It makes music," Lily said. "You just have to shake it."

Clara shook the can. "This is just noise."

"It's a percussion instrument. You'll get the hang of it."

The first cat appeared at the edge of the trees. It was followed by a dozen more.

They seemed to ripple along the ground, stalking up behind Clara. Their steps were silenced by the sand, and for whatever reason, they weren't making any of the mracking sounds he'd heard from them. Maybe after their failure bringing him down earlier, they had learned better hunting techniques.

The thought sent another shiver down his spine.

Lily could see them, too. She said, "Try again."

"This is a waste of time." Clara stepped back. Toward the trees. The treats rattled in the can as she let her arm dangle at her side.

The cats attacked.

Three leapt from the ground at the same time. Two latched onto Clara's uniform and another landed on her back, its claws digging into the fabric as it climbed higher onto her body.

"Cygnus X!" Clara yelled, spinning around.

Another cat leapt onto her arm, swatting at her gloved hand as it tried to reach the can. A fifth ran straight up her legs, perching on her shoulder and stretching toward the treats with a loud "Mrack!"

Clara screamed. She dropped the can, and tried to reach

for her plasma pistol, but her right arm was weighted down with two cats. She reached for one of them with her left hand.

This was his chance. The stasis field dropped as she shifted the hand controlling her bracer, turning her attention to the cats. Rin launched himself at her, trying to be careful to keep the cats from harm.

He caught her in the stomach, lifting her feet from the ground. The cats scattered as the pair of Sadirians hit the ground.

Rin grabbed for Clara's left hand, pinning her wrist so she couldn't activate any of the bracer's functions. He used his legs to try to block her access to the plasma pistol, but when he tightened his knees on her hips, it wasn't there.

"Freeze!"

Both of them stopped struggling at Lily's commanding shout. They looked over and saw her pointing the plasma pistol at them. Her eyes were wide and her chest was heaving with each breath. Her hands were shaking. When had she even grabbed it?

"Clara, you might want to stop struggling," Rin said.

Lily winced. "Clara?"

Shit.

"Lily," Rin said, keeping his voice gentle. "Please be careful with that."

She stepped closer. "Here, you take it."

Rin balked as she pointed the pistol's firing port right at

him. "I have to hold on to her arm to keep her from using her bracer. But, seriously, could you point that in a different direction?"

"Oh. Sure." Lily pointed the pistol at her feet.

"Not at yourself," Rin said, his heartbeat spiking. Again. "If it hits you anywhere, it'll disintegrate your entire body."

"Oh. Crap." Lily looked for a moment like she was going to just drop the pistol, but then thought better of it, thankfully.

"Okay, the first thing we're doing after this is getting you some training in how to safely handle weaponry," Rin said.

She nodded. "Yeah, that might be good."

And now, they would have a chance. Rin couldn't believe it. But with a can of cat treats and the help of Nana's glaring, they had taken down an elite Coalition soldier.

If they could do this…they could do anything.

Chapter Fifteen

"So, this is your Clara?" Lily said.

"Yeah." Rin didn't look very happy about it—or the fact that he was still having to hold Clara down. Lily didn't like that, either.

She tried not to feel a pang of envy as she took in Clara's curvy, petite figure, lustrous brown hair, and huge brown eyes. The Sadirian looked more like a pixie than a soldier. Except for the way she was glaring at Rin.

"Are you sure her emotions have been suppressed?" Lily asked. "Because she looks mad as hell."

"You're both fools," Clara said. "When I don't report back, they'll send a full team to take you into custody."

"My, she's delightful." Lily let her voice drip with sarcasm. "Maybe I can find some duct tape in the truck."

"Good idea," Rin said. "If we tape her hands together, she won't be able to use her bracer."

"Right." Lily nodded. "Bind her hands."

And strap some over her mouth.

"How do I set this ray-gun down safely?" Lily asked.

"I believe I can assist with that."

Lily turned to see Cyan approaching, a dozen cats surrounding her like an escort. She spoke a series of clicks and sibilant hisses, and half the cats sat, staring pointedly at them. The others started pacing in a circle around the group, their eyes locked on Clara.

Lily suddenly understood the word "glaring" a lot better.

"Wait a minute," Lily said. "You can talk to cats?"

"Of course I can." Cyan cocked her head at Lily. "Can't you?"

Lily let out a choppy laugh. "No."

"That is sad," Cyan said. "But perhaps I can teach you. However, I would first like to take that plasma pistol."

Cyan lifted her arm and flexed her fingers. The pistol flew from Lily's hand into Cyan's.

"Careful," Lily yelled. "That can disintegrate you."

Cyan chuckled. "I am aware of this primitive weapon's capabilities. Do not worry. I deactivated it as soon as my scans detected it."

"I thought you weren't using your exosuit," Rin said.

"Freddie came to warn me that you were in trouble." Cyan ran her hand along Freddie's spine. The cat started purring loudly again, its eyes half-closed as it pressed its head against her hip. "Circumstances demanded that I take action. I have also now disabled all technology in this soldier's uniform."

Rin let out a breath and leaned back, letting go of Clara's wrist. She shoved him away and scrambled to her feet, the sand unbalancing her footing momentarily.

Lily tried not to enjoy watching Clara flail her arms to stay upright. Tried and failed.

"You couldn't possibly…" Clara's voice trailed off as she hit one button after another on her bracer, with no effect. Her voice had lost some of its edge when she said, "I don't believe it."

"Believe what you will," Cyan said. "It will not alter your reality. Your mission has failed, along with that of the landing party that was sent to our nearby base."

"What about Montana?" Rin asked, a crease appearing between his brows.

"We have yet to make contact," Cyan said. "But we are certain our friends there will be fine. My people are en route to the *Reckoning* as we speak."

"'Your people'?" Clara sneered, but Lily could see the fear in her eyes.

"You really need to start paying more attention to the people you're oppressing," Rin said. "If any of you had bothered to talk—and listen—to the Department of Homeworld Security before launching this aggression, you would know that Earth has already formed an alliance. With the Vegans."

Lily tried not to look too smug. Clamping down on her jealousy was her second priority. Rin had called this woman "Clara", but he still hadn't confirmed that she was *that* Clara.

"This is your ex?" Lily asked.

"Yeah," Rin said.

Clara puffed up her generous chest. "Ex what?"

For someone who was supposed to have her emotions suppressed, she sure seemed upset.

She was also tiny. Somehow, hearing Rin talk about her, Lily had imagined some Amazonian warrior.

"It's just an expression," Lily said.

Clara glared at her briefly, then turned her attention to Cyan. "You claim to be a Vegan."

"I claim nothing," Cyan said. "I am stating fact. Whether you believe us or not will have no impact on the result. The High Council can not claim Earth. We will protect our new homeworld."

"This doesn't have to get ugly." Lily stepped between the two, holding Clara's gaze. "I was serious before. We can establish trade. Work out agreements. From what I've learned, your people need our help."

"Sadirians do not need help," Clara said.

Lily planted her hands on her hips. "What about the other people in the Coalition? Do you ever think of them?" She shook her head, and murmured, "Oh my God. I'm starting to sound just like Nana."

Cyan smiled up at her. "This is a good thing."

"Speaking of Nana, let's get back to her." Lily looked to Cyan, and said, "You had to use your exosuit. Do the others know about Nana and I now?"

"With the danger of the situation, I could not keep such a thing secret." Cyan bowed her head toward Rin. "I am sorry if this has unintended consequences for you."

"Don't worry about it," he said. "I knew the risks when I offered my help. Besides, this will make things better."

Lily nodded. As much as she wanted to help people, it would be easier if they could work *with* the Department of Homeworld Security instead of having to sneak around behind their back.

"Do you think they'll support our plan?" Lily said.

"Our…" Rin's eyes widened, then his lips stretched in a huge smile. "I'm starting to think anything is possible."

"The glaring and I will walk the soldier back to Lillian's house while you drive the vehicle around," Cyan said. "We will see you there shortly."

"Sounds good." Lily stepped closer to Rin, taking his hand in hers and glaring at Clara as she walked off with Cyan, surrounded by at least a dozen cats.

Neither Rin nor Lily moved toward the truck. They watched as the bizarre procession vanished through the trees. When she thought they were out of hearing range as well, Lily turned to Rin and threw her arms around his neck.

"That was terrifying," she said.

He chuckled, clasping her waist and burrowing his face in the crook of her neck. "No kidding. I can't believe how well that worked. I was sure we were getting mind-wiped or disintegrated."

"You really need to work on your optimism," Lily said.

"I guess I do. But, you know, the work is really only now beginning."

"I know."

Her dream of helping people was expanding so much more than she ever thought it could. She would trade goods that would help others, get access to technology that could help Earthlings. She just had to make sure to balance everything out and not do anything too fast or disrupt anything too much and…

She took a deep breath and let it out slowly. Maybe she needed to work on her optimism a bit, too. Staring up into Rin's eyes, it wasn't hard to imagine a future beyond all her wildest dreams.

"With you and Cyan by my side, there's nothing we can't accomplish," Lily said.

Rin smiled and leaned down to kiss her. Just before their lips met, he said, "Wait till you meet the rest of the team."

—

The *Reckoning* has arrived sooner than anyone anticipated, and the repercussions for the characters you know and love will reach farther than you think! You can learn all about it in the **double-length** *Department of Homeworld Security* book, *Coalition Reckoning*! Read on for an excerpt.

Coalition Reckoning

The Department of Homeworld Security
Book Ten

Author's note: *These events take place before, during, and after Export Duty.*

Chapter One

Rich green foliage streaked past Brigid as the helicopter wove between mountains covered in pine trees. She hadn't caught a glimpse of a city, town, or even a road for a long time.

If she wasn't so worked up over her new job, she might have tried to sleep. The jetlag from being flown all the way to Montana from Australia was murder.

"Is this the only way to reach the lodge?" She glanced over at the pilot. "By helicopter?"

He grunted, which was about as much as she'd been able to get out of the guy. At least he was nice to look at— with short dark hair, Hollywood-style jawline, and a physique that made it look like his second home was the gym.

If he was one of the people she was supposed to cook for, she'd need to refresh her memory for healthy recipes. It had been a long time since she'd had a client who was into that sort of thing, and she wasn't thinking clearly with how little sleep she'd managed on the plane.

She only felt a little bad for leaving the trial-run as executive chef for the head of one of Australia's up-and-coming production companies. The guy had been hard to pin down on any specifics, and she already wondered if his offer had been serious.

The job she was heading for was solid, immediate, and came with a ludicrous salary. Brendan only needed her for a month, and was going to pay her more than she usually earned in a year. Sitting next to the silent man-wall, she was starting to question exactly what she was getting herself into, though.

There were deep lines etched between the pilot's

eyebrows and he wore mirrored aviator glasses. From his bearing and how strongly he smelled of coffee, she had a feeling he worked security.

His button-down shirt was open enough to show off some of his chest hair. It also let her see the gnarly scar that ran over his shoulder and across his neck, disappearing beyond her view.

Maybe he was ex-military? He must have been through something terrible. She didn't understand how he could have survived such an injury.

The helicopter was raising almost as many questions as the pilot. For one, it looked way too heavy for the propeller blades to get it off the ground. Its body was made up mostly of big silver panels and thick windows that she was going to go ahead and guess were bulletproof. The landing gear things were huge and there were lights running along the length of them, unlike the simple metal bars that supported the few other helicopters she'd been this close to.

Inside, it was even more high-tech. The control panels were completely smooth, with a mix of regular dials and gauges and weird pulsing lights. Everything was the same silver metal, too—except for the barely padded black chairs. Her butt had fallen asleep ten minutes after take-off.

"I like the design etched on the panel." She reached out to run her finger over the ivy-like pattern.

The pilot grabbed her arm in a grip so tight it nearly hurt. He looked over at her and finally spoke.

"Don't. Touch. Anything," he said.

"My bad."

He let go of her arm, then ran a finger over one of the patterns. The etchings lit up, and the helicopter made a few beeping noises.

Shoot, are those part of the controls?

Brigid looked around more carefully, folding her hands in her lap and pulling her legs closer to the chair in an effort to not accidentally bump into anything.

A glass and metal dome appeared amid the foliage, with three large spans of roof spreading out from it. If this was the lodge, it was the strangest mix of futuristic and rustic she'd ever seen.

Finally.

They swung around and hovered over a small landing pad before setting down. She couldn't wait to stretch her legs—and to get out of this thing.

A tall, thin man with red hair and a neatly trimmed beard was standing off to the side of where they landed. He was wearing jeans and a burgundy sweater.

There was a woman next to him who was almost as tall as he was. She was absolutely stunning, with a huge smile on her supermodel-perfect face. Her hair was blonde, and she was dressed similarly, but her sweater was a clashing mish-mash of colors that no fashionista would be caught dead in.

Under her breath, Brigid said, "Yikes."

"Just wait."

The pilot couldn't have heard her, could he?

The engine noises weren't lessening, though they were quieter than she'd expected. They hadn't even needed those oversized headphones people always wore in movies when they rode in helicopters.

The red-head trotted up to the helicopter, ducking low under the propellers. One of the side doors in the back opened automatically.

As soon as he was inside, he said, "Hi, I'm Brendan."

This was her new boss? He was cuter than she'd expected, especially when he smiled at her. He reached into the cockpit to shake her hand awkwardly.

"Nice to meet you," she said. "I'm Brigid."

Brendan chuckled. "I know."

"Right." Of course he knew. He'd hired her and sent this man-wall to come get her.

Brendan turned to the pilot, and said, "Zemanni, turn off the engine."

"No." The pilot—Zemanni—shook his head. "Take your passenger and get out."

Wow.

So much for this guy being one of Brendan's security guards. She couldn't imagine anyone tolerating that kind of attitude from a subordinate.

At least Zemanni was rude to everyone and not just her. She'd been wondering if she had offended him somehow.

What the heck kind of name is 'Zemanni' anyway?

"You're not coming in?" Brendan smirked, obviously baiting the pilot. "Everyone will be so *torn up* to miss you."

Brigid didn't get the joke, and Zemanni didn't seem to find it funny. He turned to glare at Brendan. The lights from the dashboard were doing some weird reflecting thing on the white scar tissue around Zemanni's neck, because it almost looked like it was glowing.

"Get out," Zemanni repeated. "Or I'll take her back with me and you'll have to keep eating Dane's cooking."

Brendan's smirk faded. He nodded at Brigid and said, "We'd better go."

"Oh, sure." She managed to unbuckle her safety harness and climb into the main cabin of the helicopter with Brendan. He picked up two of her bags, leaving her backpack for her to grab.

The moment their feet hit the white concrete of the landing pad, the door behind them slid shut. The trill of the engine increased, but was drowned out by a high, screeching roar that echoed through the forest. Brigid had never heard anything like it. She ducked down, heart pounding, scanning the trees and sky.

"What was that?" she said.

"That?" Brendan shrugged. "Probably a bear."

"A bear?" Her voice was shrill. She realized she wasn't using the best tone with her new boss, but couldn't help herself.

The helicopter took off.

Craaaap.

"There is no way that was a bear," Brigid said.

Brendan straightened as soon as the helicopter lifted off, and smiled down at her. "I thought I hired a chef, not a zoologist."

"My sister is a veterinarian." A familiar sense of pride flooded her chest, followed by just a little bit of envy.

Caitlin worked with all kinds of animals. She even assisted park rangers when they needed help with wildlife in the area around their home town in Arizona.

Cooking could be important, too, but Brigid mainly catered to people who were just seeking entertainment or distraction. Her experiments in molecular gastronomy were the only accomplishments she was really proud of. The people she'd worked for had always seemed more interested in showing off her cuisine than actually enjoying it. It was all politics and posturing.

"I didn't know she'd been trained in identifying bear calls," Brendan said.

He talked almost as if he'd already known what Caitlin did. Brigid was used to people checking references when she started a new job, but they usually didn't dig into her family.

She thought about the helicopter again and the military-looking guy who piloted it. Maybe she was going to have a chance to do something more meaningful after all.

The blonde woman approached them and took one of the bags from Brendan.

"It sounded more like a mountain lion to me." The woman extended her free hand toward Brigid. "I'm Vay. It's wonderful to meet you."

"You…too." Brigid was still giving most of her attention to the thick foliage around them. And crouching, she realized, as she looked up at Vay. Brigid forced herself to stand and tried to unbunch her shoulders. "Do you get many mountain lions around here?"

"Not really," Vay said.

"Then why do you think that was a mountain lion?" Brigid asked.

Vay opened her mouth, then shut it again and smiled, the skin around her eyes crinkling.

At least she wasn't afraid. Brendan seemed unfazed as well.

"We should probably head inside," Vay said.

"That's a great idea." Brendan gestured toward the house. "After you."

What the heck have I gotten myself into?

—

About the Author

USA Today Bestselling author Cassandra Chandler uses her vivid imagination to make the world more interesting, spawning the ideas she turns into her whimsical Science Fiction romcoms and darkly evocative Paranormal and Urban Fantasy Romances. Fast-paced and funny, lighthearted or dark, her stories will introduce you to characters you want to be friends with and worlds where you'd like to build a vacation home.